P9-DGS-838
3 9077 08826 2087
RANDOM HOUSE
LARGE PRINT
LARGE PRINT
AUG - 3 2020
BEN
Bender, Aimee
The Butterfly Lampshade

The Butterfly Lampshade

The Butterfly Lampshade

A NOVEL

Aimee Bender

Published in the United States of America by Random House Large Print in association with Doubleday, a division of Penguin Random House LLC, New York.

Cover art based on a photograph by so_illustrator/Getty Images
Cover art and design by Emily Mahon

The Library of Congress has established a Cataloging-in-Publication record for this title.

ISBN: 978-0-593-34209-1

www.penguinrandomhouse.com/large-print-format-books

FIRST LARGE PRINT EDITION

Printed in the United States of America

10 9 8 7 6 5 4 3 2 1

This Large Print edition published in accord with the standards of the N.A.V.H.

for HD

I'm still asleep,
but meanwhile facts are taking place.

—Wisława Szymborska, "Early Hour"

PART ONE

Tent

1

We cannot tend to her. There is something wrong with her.

What do you mean? What is wrong with her?

We do not know. Something.

She seems like such a normal little girl to me. Last visit—

It is hidden.

Did she do anything? Did she do something bad?

No.

Then what?

We cannot handle her. I cannot.

But what do you mean by that? Is she misbehaving?

No.

Is she getting in trouble in school?

You have to come get her.

I don't understand.

You are the godparents. You have to come. That is your job.

But you are alive, Elaine.

The Butterfly Lampshade

I am telling you I can't do it.

Where's that new guy you were telling me about?

Camping.

Is he coming back?

I don't know.

Are you going to do something, Elaine?

I could call social services. Maybe I will. Are they listed? Will they do foster care if other family is still available?

Can you put her on the phone?

No.

Is she nearby?

She's right here. She's looking right at me.

Can you tell her to come on the phone?

Francie. Francie, dear, your aunt Minnie wants to speak to you.

Hello? Francie?

Hello.

Francie? Are you okay?

Yes.

You've been listening to our conversation?

Yes.

Your mother is very worried about you. Do you think you might be doing anything wrong?

No.

Have you been going to school?

Yes.

Are you behaving properly in school?

Yes.

Are you going to bed on time?

Yes.

I have to tell you, I'm more worried about your mother. Do you think she might be getting sick again?

Yes.

Can you tell me what she's doing?

No.

You can tell me. I know she's probably listening, but it's okay. Really. She knew I would ask you. Is she hurting you in any way, any way at all?

No.

Is she—dressed?

Yes.

Okay. That's good. Are you feeling okay?

Yes.

Do you need me to come up there?

Yes.

Yes?

Yes.

Can you tell me what you mean by yes? As in why?

No.

Is your mom's friend there?

No.

He's out of town?

I don't know.

Is anyone else there?

No.

Is your mother hurting herself?

No.

Sweetie, I'm so sorry, I just can't come this time,

not right now. I'm too pregnant. I'm not allowed to go on a plane. Your uncle can, though. You want your uncle to come?

No.

Oh, Francie. Who is the best grown-up for you to call?

It's me again, Minn. She dropped the phone. She's standing by the wall now. She puts her nose right up against the wall. It's touching the wall.

What is happening over there?

Like she is talking to the wall. She has this look, Minn.

Kids have looks.

No, no. Other kids don't have this look.

Elaine, she can hear the whole conversation for God's sake!

Like she is judging me. All the time.

Kids don't judge, not like that.

She does.

You're still on the Abilify?

I cannot be around her. There's something in her. There is a bug in her. I cannot even trust myself around her! Are you listening to me?

Yes. I'm sending Stan up. The minute he gets home. Morning flight.

Not Stan! You!

I can't fly. What do you mean, a bug?

A bug in her. Something crawling inside her.

Can she stay somewhere else? Where can she stay?

I don't know.

A friend?

I don't like her friends.

A friend of yours?

She loves her babysitter.

Ask the babysitter. Of course. Tomorrow. Or, I'll call her too. We can both call her. Okay? This is the one who also works at the school?

Shrina.

I have her number. We'll work something out, honey. You have to call your doctor. We'll both call the doctor.

I know I should. I know I do.

And I will too. So that's a start. We have a plan then.

We do?

We'll both make some calls in the morning. Okay? Let's go over the plan. What are you going to do tomorrow?

I am going to call my doctor.

Good. And?

I am going to call my doctor.

And, if you feel able, ask the babysitter.

Right. And I will ask the babysitter.

What are you going to ask the babysitter?

If she will take my sweet girl, Francie. But what do I mean again? Where will she take her?

You know what, I'll call Shrina. Don't worry about that. You take care of yourself. Maybe Francie can stay with her for a couple days while we get you feeling better. Do you know where she lives?

She is very young.

Francie?

The babysitter.

It's just until Stan can get up there. I'll tell her he'll be coming as soon as he can.

How many months are you again?

Eight and a half. So that's the plan for tomorrow. But what about tonight?

Tonight? Exactly!

Does she have a lock on her door?

Her bedroom door? Yes. She does. She asked for that.

What do you mean? She asked for a lock?

Last year. For her birthday.

You're kidding me. Did she ask for anything else?

Is that odd?

Just a lock?

Yes.

Unbelievable. But okay. She's a smart girl. It's very useful. From the inside?

Yes.

And how about you?

We can both lock our doors from the inside.

Okay. You need to do that then. Why don't you do that as soon as we get off the phone. Use the bathroom first. Then go to bed. You'll call me tomorrow morning?

Yes.

You'll call the doctor?

Yes.

You'll call me if you need anything, absolutely anything?

Yes.

Tell Francie goodbye. Tell her I love her.

You're on speaker. She can hear you.

Jesus. Goodbye, Francie. Did you hear that about locking your door?

Yes.

I love you, Francie.

She doesn't say I love you.

I will say it anyway. She doesn't have to say it back. I love you, Francie.

Goodbye, Minn. Thank you so much. I love you.

I love you too, Elaine. We'll figure this out.

Thank you. I love you.

I love you too, Elaine. Go to your room now, honey. Good night.

2

My mother had placed a tape recorder in every room of our apartment. They were cheap and easy to find at secondhand stores, as were the tapes. When she brought them home, she tried to hide them by placing one piece of folded white paper over each device like a little tent. Each room, with its white paper tent. She had started buying them weeks before that phone conversation with Aunt Minn, and when we were in a room together, she would casually drift over to the tent and sneak a finger underneath to find a button and press Record. Then she'd make breakfast, or play cards with me, or we'd watch **Toy Story 2,** or I'd do my homework. I understood implicitly that they were not to be discussed, that I was to think the little white tent was an actual cover, and her pressing of the button invisible to me. I suppose I liked the idea of a shared secret, even if she did not know I shared it. In fact, had she looked carefully, my mother might've seen a few more white tents on appliances in my bedroom as a tribute: a white piece of paper over the clock radio, a white piece of paper folded over a broken camera. This field of tents, this camping ground of our home. In the other rooms, we would play our games and eat our meals, and I grew used to the rubbery click of a cassette running out, a button upending as the closing point of most activities. At some point, while I was at school, or asleep, she must've flipped the tapes, but I never saw that part. They were always prepped and ready to go. When the volunteer mothers from my school were packing up the apartment and going through her and my things, they mentioned nothing to Aunt Minn about any bag full of labeled cassettes, any grand plan documentary, which was not a surprise; Mom just wasn't generally that organized. I never ended up asking her about them, but it didn't seem like a long-term project. More like she wanted some proof in case I did something bad. And, as I think of it now, probably keeping an ear on herself, too.

Before those volunteer mothers arrived, when I was gathering a few of my own things to take with me before I went to live with my aunt and uncle in their home in Burbank, California, I lifted each little tent like the boxtop of a present and took the tape recorders, slid each one into my purple drawstring bag along with a stuffed brown bunny I didn't really care about and some word search books in which I had already found all the words. I had no idea what to bring. The scrim of meaning had floated off of everything.

I brought the recorders with me on the train for two days, and then into the car and up the walkway to my new home, on the quiet street of well-tended lawns and a bright blue tire swing across the road hanging from the gnarled branch of an oak tree. Supposedly, when I rang the doorbell, and my aunt answered, holding a tiny fretting brand-new infant in her arms, hair frizzed, face etched, I pointed to myself and said, "Francie." "It was the most heartbreaking thing in the world," she told me years later, pressing my hand, "as if we were acquaintances at a party."

That morning, she hugged and kissed me as she led me up the stairs. My room was to be at the top of the staircase, with windows that looked out upon the street, and a faint odor of yoga mats. It had been previously used as an exercise room and an office, and so all the equipment had been shoved to one side, shrouded by a few old green sheets, and by the closet they'd set up a futon draped in a too-large comforter and a nightstand made of a packing box covered by a towel. She had no spare reading lamp, so she'd placed an industrial flashlight on the towel in case I liked to read at night.

"I'm so sorry," she said, bouncing the baby, who was wrapped in a blanket. "We'll get this into shape. We just have been so consumed."

"I like the flashlight," I said.

"We'll go online. We'll order whatever you like."

"What is the baby's name?" I asked, still standing in the doorframe.

She blushed. Her eyes seemed to have constant water in them, a vivid hydrated health. She looked nothing like my mother. "Vicky," she said. "Your cousin Vicky. Or, maybe—your sister?"

"Cousin is good," I said, holding out a finger, which the baby grabbed.

Months later, after extensive shopping, once I was settled in my new room, with its yellow skirt on the bed, and cloud-painted lamp, and painting of rainbows perched on clouds on the wall, and art table, and cardboard dollhouse, on an afternoon when I had nothing to do, I emptied the purple drawstring bag of its devices, inserted a tape, and pressed Play on the one from the Bathroom, and then the Kitchen. I had been missing my mother very much, but it turned out I couldn't stand listening. Hearing my squeaky voice, hearing hers. The cracking of eggs for breakfast, her laughing as she brushed her teeth and sang me a song about spitting. The dim sounds of Go Fish. The conversation from the Living Room recorder between us all was the only one I could listen to in full, because it was the last I had, and the easiest to rewind to, and didn't cause the same kind of ache.

3

I don't know whether there is a lot of documentation on psychotic people and psychic people and if they have any overlap. I'm guessing no. Most people in the grip of psychosis are not usually considered trusted custodians of the future. The man at the bus stop warning us all about the end of the world has been there since its beginning, since there were bus stops to stand by, or their bygone equivalents, like the horse trading station. There he was, by a pile of hay, yelling of brimstone, and no one paid him much mind then either.

But it turned out that my mother was right about the bug. She was several days too early, and mine had not been crawling, but there would end up being a bug in me after all, just a few days after she checked into the hospital, my fated bug, a butterfly I'd found at the babysitter's apartment, floating like a red and gold leaf so prettily on the top of a tall glass of water. I did not have any other way to hold on to it, and I could not possibly leave it in the babysitter's apartment, and the only container handy was myself. Time was short. I drank it down because I had to.

4

The night after the locked bedrooms, my mother had knocked on my door in the early morning.

"You can come out," she said. "I'm better."

Her voice, back to its consoling musicality, singsongy and light. I ducked my head through the doorway, and she hugged me, and petted my hair, and told me I was a beautiful girl. "There is a bug in me," I said, and she said no, "no, no. Don't listen to me. Darling! Don't. I was in crazy mode. Don't listen. There is a bug in **me**." "Not you," I said. Her hair was brushed, and smelled of the sweet lemon hair product she used to comb it through. She was wearing her most special bathrobe, a gift from Aunt Minn, the one with the red satin edging and an eruption of ruffles at the neck. We went to the kitchen as per our usual morning routine and ate fried eggs and toast together, and then after I'd filled the pan with soapy water, and dressed and brushed my teeth, she sat with me on the damp cement second-story stoop to wait for Alberta's mother, who drove me to school because she'd apparently heard rumors about my mother from someone else at the elementary school, and Alberta's mother decided she did not want to put Alberta in our car for a carpool, so one day she'd volunteered to do it all.

Outside, it was foggy and gray, the promise of a late morning rain, early March on the Willamette.

"Are you going to ask the babysitter?" I asked. The babysitter, Shrina, came over only occasionally, but when she did, she would march into our apartment with a tote bag packed with construction paper and glitter and glue sticks, like some kind of art fairy.

My mother glanced at me. She touched a finger to the edge of her lips, like she was trying to remember something.

"If I should stay with her," I said.

"You don't need to stay with anyone else."

"Are you going to call your doctor?"

"I'm feeling much better today."

Across the street, a neighbor walked by, tugged by two small white dogs. Below us, the stairway zigzagged down, and toward the bottom, what looked like a silverfish turned off a step to shimmer into a clamor of ferns.

"Aunt Minnie probably already called her," I said.

"I'll talk to your aunt later."

Alberta's mother drove up in their burgundy car. Alberta was sitting in the back. She pressed a paper doll of an army soldier up against the window. Her father was off in another country, for war purposes.

"Bye," I told my mother.

She kissed my cheek and told me to have a wonderful day.

"Make it a fun one," she said. "Will you do that for me?"

I nodded as I headed down the steps. It was just like her to sever her mood from the day like that, as if she had no impact on me.

If I piece together the timing, she shattered her hand with a hammer less than an hour later, because, she told the doctor, she'd been overcome by the notion that there was something crawling inside her bones and she wanted to see it. "Or smash it," she told the doctor, who told my aunt. "You know. The way you smash a spider." "But who hits spiders with a hammer?" my aunt whispered to my uncle, in their hallway, after she'd gotten off the phone in the kitchen with the hospital psychiatrist. By then, I had been at their home for about a week. The hallway walls were interposed with tiny framed embroideries of farm animals that she'd found on a cheese trip to Vermont and thought were the sweetest pictures she'd ever seen. They were very sweet. They were also kind of hard to see, they were that small. On occasion, with little else to do, I would drag over a stool to determine if one was a lamb, or a goat. "You're applying regular logic," my uncle murmured back. "What makes sense about any of this?" and my aunt shook her head in hard little movements and when I got up the nerve to scoot past them from my outpost in the kitchen, she was leaning heavily on his chest, eyes closed. Where was baby Vicky? In some wheeled hooded contraption bound by a blanket.

With her functional hand, my mother managed to call 911, who sent an ambulance, treated her for shock, then broken bones, and once stable in the hospital, directed her to the psych ward, where they declared her in the midst of another psychotic episode and unfit for parenting. My uncle hopped on the next flight to Portland. My aunt, who had spent the morning calling first the babysitter and then hospitals after getting no answer on the home line, went into labor a couple weeks early, and after my uncle landed, he drove in from the airport, ran up the steps of my school like a man in a movie, folded me into his arms, and then took out a pad of paper and set everything up before flying home to be back as close to the birth of his own daughter as possible. I believe he missed Vicky's entry into the world but was there for the first feeding. In the front office, he knelt and asked me to come with him that day, to "join us, to be with all of us for this big moment," but I refused to go because a) it was still brand-new information that I would be leaving town, and b) I didn't see him/them all that often, and c) I would not take a plane. "I will scream," I said, by the office's long wooden waiting bench, surrounded by concerned-looking secretaries, beneath a series of sunset-themed watercolors as produced by one of the other grades. "I will scream, and then I will stop, and then I will scream again." I said it simply, but I had eyes that could fix on an adult and I knew how to hold a gaze without blinking. His own eyes, fluttering open and closed, looked tired, rimmed with red.

"It's true," piped in the head administrator, Mrs. Washington, with her brilliant pink lipstick, pausing at her keyboard. "She has been frightened of planes all year."

I was eight years old then, and we'd had a transportation unit as part of our curriculum that year, on buses, trains, planes, bikes. I'd been so afraid of the airplane section that the teacher had allowed me to do extra work on locomotion instead, including an interview with this same Mrs. Washington in the front office, whose brother was a conductor on the rail line from Atlanta to D.C. I had assumed at the time, despite reassurance, that a plane flew so fast you could only see blur out the window, and what I needed in those days more than almost anything was to track where I was and where I was going. In this way, I could feel myself and my priorities as very different from those of other children. Mrs. Washington told me all about her brother's role on the train, his seat in the front, his engineering degree, and all the stops—eighteen—including one in Charlotte, which was the name of one of my classmates, and I wrote up my report and attached an extensive illustration and was done with it.

But the need to track my existence didn't end there; sometimes, at recess, while other kids slid and swung and hurled themselves joyfully through space, I would stand by myself at the far end of the playground, and hold still to take stock of my physical cutout in the world. It was a way to remind myself of myself, to tap into the world outside: feet on pavement, taste of cracker, silver fence, breezy air, and it was a very useful activity for me, if alienating to others. I did not, to my luck, catch the eye of the deep bullies, so all I got called was Statue or Lump or teased because Freeze Tag had ended long ago, and a classmate might groan, "Will someone please unfreeze Francie?" while running back to class after the bell rang, and someone might just listen, tapping my shoulder as they passed, and I would use that little link, that beautiful wrong context to pull me back from far inside myself to the group of humanness to which they said I belonged. I usually felt so much better then, following them in, clattering into the classroom, so much surer after taking stock that I could settle in my seat and thank the red cheeks and shining eyes of Luther or Janie or whoever had freed me, and we all laughed at my outer-spaciness even though it had been the pure opposite, that my usual performance of social participation was in fact far more subject to internal drift than the me who stood by herself with eyes closed listening to others play. When my mother, on the phone with her sister, had watched me standing so close to the wall and thought I was talking to it or bonding with it, all I had been doing was a version of the same thing, feeling where my nose made contact with wall, feeling edge of skin meet plaster, and thus finding myself in the difference. My great love then—and still—is delineation. A plane, and possible blur, was out of the question.

"Train," I said, looking at my uncle right in the eye.

"It will take two days."

"Okay."

"I can't go with you."

"That is fine. I can take it alone," and he laughed with soft bitterness and said he'd find me some kind of steward. He thanked the secretaries and led me outside, into the slate-skied afternoon.

By this point, it was just past school lunchtime, and across the street, the local cafés and eateries were filling up with neighborhood adults. We stood by the cement base of the flagpole and watched them for a while as they entered their restaurants, me absorbing his nervous, kindly presence. He smelled of peppermints and sweat. The last time I'd seen my uncle here in Portland was many months earlier, during the Fourth of July holiday weekend, when he and my aunt had flown up to visit and my mother had presented them with four crocheted blankets at the airport of varying shades of red, white, and blue that she'd knitted during a stretch of sleepless nights. I would get a full night's rest and wake up and the house would have birthed a new blanket. The closet overflowed with them. A few had skipped stitches you could stick an arm through, and I took those to be like visual representations of her speeded-up mind, when she was going so fast she could hardly stay in her chair, which made me crumple inside, thinking of it, but that also (now) I find weirdly touching realizing how hard she was working not to get me up. At the airport, by the baggage claim, when my aunt had widened her eyes like a terrified deer, seeing the giant bag with blanket after blanket emerging, like the bag was vomiting blankets, my mother laughed in a shrill way and grabbed two back right away. "Kidding!" she laughed. "Just kidding! These are for the school blanket drive." Her eyes flashed, and she wrapped the striped one around herself as if to hold herself together. She had told me once while tucking me in that she did not always know when her behavior was off, which was one of the more horrifying aspects of being sick, she said, that she did not always know what was well, and what was sick, and she had asked me, please, to tell her. "Please." The colorful bar sign from down the street had turned on and cast a grid of reddish light on her cheek so she looked like a person in a movie, eyes pleading, a lit tear traversing the frames. I patted her hand,

and lied, and told her of course I would, no problem. On that airport morning, my aunt's face had stepped in and done the job for all of us.

At the flagpole, in front of the elementary school, my uncle and I stood together like we had never seen people enter restaurants before, people holding the door for one another, settling into seats to read menus. People sitting at the window, drinking from glasses of water. People talking, and shaking salt onto piles of food behind reflections of cloud movement in the grand picture windows. We stood for over fifteen minutes, and I made no move in any direction. Other than the hard line about not taking the plane, my will was pap. When, earlier in the day, during a lesson on the color wheel, the principal had summoned me out of class to her office to stare at me behind thick black-framed plastic glasses and tell me what had happened, which she hardly understood, and I hardly understood, what I had been able to grasp almost instantly, besides a dull awareness of a surprising amount of blue paperweights in her office, and the flashing red dome light of her industrial phone, was that I would not likely be able to live at home anymore. After all, I had heard the phone conversation the night before. I had been living with her, and just her, for years. The man she'd been seeing was only an occasional kind of beau, who would vanish after this event, never to be seen again. I was surprised, and trembling, and wrecked, and nauseated, but not particularly shocked.

"Can I see her?" I asked my uncle, as we crossed the street and settled into a swirly painted booth at the busy burrito place that smelled strongly of cinnamon horchata. He said no, not for a while.

"She is very sick, Francie."

"Will her hand heal?"

"Her hand will heal."

"Will her head heal?"

"Her head will heal, too, but more slowly."

I thought about that. "Is there a bug in her?" I asked.

My uncle rubbed his face, and then picked up a pastel-colored sugar packet. "No," he said, wringing the paper until it burst. "Sort of," he said.

Our food arrived, and he lifted his burrito over a bed of glittering sugar crystals, while I opened mine to find the circle of tortilla containing it, because one might not remember that the lumpy burrito bundle had been built from such a shape.

"She was able to make me eggs this morning," I said as we wandered back to the school, and he nodded, hands deep in his pockets. "She put the eggshells in the trash. She took out the trash last week and put it in the bin."

"That's good," he said, bobbing his head, obviously elsewhere. "That bodes well for her recovery." He looked at his phone for the nth time and called my aunt, who proclaimed, so loud I could hear it, that she was seven centimeters. "She says she loves you," he told me, hanging up, even though she had said no such thing. We crossed the school lawn and found our way to a different classroom, now empty of kids, where my babysitter also worked as a teacher's aide, and he explained the situation across a congregation of tiny orange chairs and asked if there was any possible chance that maybe I could stay with her for a couple days while he set things up for the train trip. "I'm so sorry to impose," he said. "She just loves you very much." The babysitter knelt and hugged me. We had not spent loads of time together, but I had cherished every moment with her. She was fun, and kind, and had these huge obsidian eyes, so beautiful they seemed to be filled from some magical source of lava inside her and when a tear dripped from the corner of her eye I was honestly surprised it was clear. "Your wife called this morning," she told him, nodding. "I think it would be okay. We'll have a little sleepover. My place is small, though!" "I'm small," I said, and she laughed, lightly. "It's true. You are small." "She is small," echoed my uncle, not a tall man, and she bowed her head, as if we were elves.

5

When I was old enough to travel back to Portland by myself, nearly ten years later, I took the plane up to visit my mother in the residential facility where she had moved, and now lived. My mother had stayed—and still stays—in the same place she transferred to after the hospital so many years ago, a two-level sprawling building called Hawthorne House located in the southeast quadrant of the city, and it was a very good choice, a desired option with a wait list and excellent ratings. They'd primarily built it for the elderly, but sometimes also took the mentally ill as it was a fairly large facility and they were eager to fill beds. I had been there many, many times since my move, sometimes a few times a year, but always accompanied by my aunt and/or uncle. This was to be my first trip solo.

I consider this visit my earliest real attempt to make some sense of the unusual events that had happened while I was leaving Portland to move to Los Angeles. That it failed so plainly may be part of the reason it has taken me so long to look at it all again.

The trip was planned for a Saturday to make it easier for everyone. I would fly up in the morning and return on the last flight of the day, home by nine p.m., as usually happened when I flew up with my aunt or uncle. This way we saved the money we would've spent on a hotel, and it kept the visit short, and focused.

On the day of my flight, at five-thirty in the morning, seventeen years old, I went downstairs to find the humming motor and brilliant headlights of Aunt Minn's car in the driveway already waiting to take me to the airport. She was sitting quietly in profile in the driver's seat, eyes weary, cardigan soft around her shoulders. I hadn't heard much of her getting ready in the house, just soft movement through rooms like a wraith, and some whispers to Uncle Stan from their doorway that seemed related to getting Vicky breakfast even though she would probably be back before Vicky was even awake. We lived so close to the Burbank Airport, and Vicky was sound asleep, her door cracked open to let in the light from the hall. The rest of the house was dark. Shuttling patterns of tree leaves moved over the windows as if it were the middle of the night. As we drove away from the house and turned the corner onto Magnolia, the streets opened up before us, straight and empty, drained of cars, the shadowy lumps of the Verdugo Mountains faintly visible in the near distance.

It had been my idea to go up on my own. I was soon to enter my senior year of high school, and my mother had, a few weeks earlier, tried to leave Hawthorne House to take me back, even though the timing made no sense, and I had never agreed to go, but she had returned to the facility after a few days anyway, apologizing to me at every phone call, voice crashing about how she just couldn't do it, she was so sorry, that Hawthorne House was better for her right now but that she would hopefully be able to try again soon. This was all her own conversation with herself; I had no plan to move back up there, which I had never said to her out loud, but I'd decided as a kind of compromise that maybe I could fly up on my own for the first time, just to see her for the afternoon. Vicky was doing a bug project related to her summer art/science camp, including all kinds of materials and drawings, and it had sparked my own interest in retelling Vicky about the emergence of the butterfly, as well as the next visitor, the beetle that had soon followed, and I'd thought, as she and I cut out spider bodies from black cardstock, attaching twisted pipe cleaner antennae, threading ants from brown beads, for the first time, that it actually might also be helpful to talk about these incidences with my mother. Maybe she would have some ideas. Maybe she, in fact, was the perfect person to help me give this strangeness its due. I definitely didn't want to trouble Aunt Minn, who took any unordinary conversation as worrisome bait that my mind might be turning.

That evening, spiders tucked leggily into Vicky's shoebox, after I'd helped out in the kitchen and Vicky was settled into bed, Uncle Stan out on an errand getting paper towels, I had approached my aunt at the desk in her room where she sat returning work emails. Her and my uncle's bedroom sparkled with its array of delicates, including a daisy-encrusted glass cube, a hammered tin sign telling her to **Slow Down** in raised cursive, the old clay pen cup I'd made years ago that my mother had sent her once as a gift from Portland. "Come in, Francie!" she said, seeing me there. "Please! I could use a little distraction." At her desk, I told her I wanted her advice, that I knew we were due for our late summer Portland visit, but that I was thinking I might like to fly up to see my mother on my own this time, just to give it a try, my voice so tentative, fingers twisting, and her face, strained by work details, had cleared, and opened; "Oh, I'm sure she'd love that!" she said, laughing with delight, and she clicked away from her tasks, and went onto the airline's website right away so we could pick out the flight together. Her presence next to me, firm, excited, confident in the idea, was the only reason I could select my seats, and input her credit card number, and get the confirmation email; besides the obvious and crucial financial support, her body by mine was supplying an interim space in which the buying of this plane ticket was possible.

To my surprise, I looked forward to the trip for weeks. I usually did not enjoy our visits to Portland; good rating or not, I didn't like the facility, with its nurses briskly walking everywhere, and the rusting outdoor furniture, and my pulse rushing when we turned the corner to find my mother waiting for us with giant eyes like we'd long been separated at sea. But this time felt different, driven by something new, and my mother, on the Sunday calls, had bubbled over with excitement when I'd told her, and had talked nonstop about how there would be a special space next to her at lunch, and that she was making me a sweater, and that she wanted to introduce me to everyone the minute I stepped in from the airport. Plus, the plane itself, what had tormented me at eight years old, was no longer an issue. Turned out the adults had been right, and it did not blur out the window after all. Years earlier, when my aunt and I had flown up together to see my mother for the first time, just a few months after the move to Burbank, I had gripped her hand in our cushioned seats, terrified, knuckles tight, and Aunt Minn had pulled the shade over her window while I kept my head down and tried to focus on my activity book. As I worked, I kept checking my hands to see if they would blur, if I was already dissipating, and once in a moment of courage let my eyes graze to the window across the aisle in the other direction, expecting to find a world that had lost definition, but the landscape was sharply drawn and particulate below, as if we were not traveling hundreds of miles per hour, and I found I could track all of it—tidy patterns of farmland, gray strips of road, mountain crevices, cloud movement. The flight attendant came by with a cart, and he was clear too, a person with outlines, and the orange juice he handed to me looked like any other orange juice I ever drank on firm land. So the ride was good, and Aunt Minn had hugged me with pride when we landed, telling me how I had conquered a fear, which was by far the best part of the visit, because that time at Hawthorne House itself had been rough. My mother, at that stage, knew no one at the facility except one doctor and two nurses, and she'd wept onto Minn's shoulder, her face small with helplessness and loss, the two sisters holding each other tightly, while I'd stood and stared with a kind of rabid intensity at the pointillated seascapes on the walls.

"Anything I should look out for with Mom?" I asked, at seventeen, when we stopped at a red light near Victory, the only car in the intersection. The darkness was beginning to thin around us, although the sun had not yet peeked out from behind the hills. My aunt shook her head. She said she didn't think so. Just to enjoy myself, truly. Her eyes were alert and sad on the road, focused on the traffic light, and she felt, on that morning, of a particular mystery to me. The light changed, and we passed rows of stores like movie sets, modest cobblers, and cafés, and burger joints, progressing through the streets, moving into Burbank's everlasting supply of parts stores: sheet metal, vinyl, fiberglass, door and window showrooms. A few cars joined us on the street, headlights dazzling, and the outlines of hills began to sharpen a little in the distance. When the glowing sign for the airport rose up on our left, Bob Hope Airport, named for the actor who had lived his adult life nearby in Toluca Lake, Aunt Minn pulled to the curb at Terminal 1, handing over a white bakery bag of cookies my mother liked, an anise version of a biscotti almost certainly also available in Portland. My aunt brought this bag on our trip every time. Apparently long ago, in childhood, my mother had loved dipping biscotti.

"I'll pick you up at nine," Aunt Minn said, kissing my cheek. "It will mean so much for her to see you by yourself."

And then she waved goodbye, pulling into the exit lane, leaving me at the edge of the sidewalk with the sun now stretching its morning rays to illuminate the browning slopes and tangled orange moss of the mountains. A few people trickled in from the parking lot with sheet-lined faces and damp hair, and the man outside at the gate drummed his fingers on the counter, waiting to check bags for passengers who did not want to check their bags indoors. I went inside to print my boarding pass and walked to security, which was empty. I was the only person in my line. The security officers were joking with each other about their Friday night pursuits, and I went through the motions, shoes off, shoes on, arms up, arms down, until my bag passed the X-ray and they waved me through, and all the while, as I advanced through the checkpoints, I tried to manage what felt like an almost crushing surge of anticipation inside, imagining myself alone with her, my mother.

It had been, by that point, almost ten years since I'd moved away from Portland, and therefore almost ten years since I had been with my mother by myself. Usually, on these visits, I felt myself as an appendage, following my aunt's lead; she led the question and answer with my mother in the old lime green silk chairs in the main living room area, and she arranged the meal; she knew the nurses by name, and reported to my mother news of my good grades and jobs and modest accomplishments. I was relieved to let her do all of it, and usually sat next to her, braiding the soft tassels of the brocade pillows, nodding, listening, understanding my job as visitor as being made up of two parts—one, to privately manage the overwhelm of sense memory and longing and coldness I always felt seeing my mother again, and two, through my live presence, to show the other residents I existed, and that the smiley photos in frames in her room were therefore not cut from magazines. Every time I had previously stepped into Hawthorne House, my mother ran over and hugged me and clasped my hands and shouted "Francie!" in a voice heavy with feeling, and claiming, telling me how much she missed me, and how she had been looking at flights and would be coming to see me soon, so soon, usually adding something about Disneyland. None of this was true; or, she may very well have been looking at flights, but she had never been able to visit, and she still said it every time as if the act of saying it was a kind of version of it, a visit in words. Neither of us could seem to admit aloud that we lived in different cities, and had, by that point, for a long time. Those weeks back, when she had checked out on the provisional pause to try to live on her own again, she had forgotten to take her medication, and within a week had returned, as they had a psychiatrist checking in, and the decline was obvious, and likely deliberate. This board and care was one of the better facilities in the city that accepted her Medicare, and no one really wanted her to give up her spot. No one meaning my aunt and my uncle, and possibly her, and surely, at times, me.

The keepers of the gate called my category, B 1–30, and I exited the glass door to the open air of the paved runway edges, mounting the movable staircase to enter the body of the plane and take my seat. As usual, I could see my mother in my mind as a dot on a map, far up the coast, and as I did the sudoku puzzle in the airline magazine, and drank my orange juice, and ate my peanuts, I moved through the air toward her, soaring over clouds past cities, and agriculture, and coastlines. I could track all of it. Everything so crisp to the eye. On the ground, I took the Red Line all the way to City Center, transferring to the 71, and then finally, near Fiftieth, walked several blocks through some blooming rhododendron-full residential streets up to the door of Hawthorne House, where I showed my ID at the front desk and told them I was there to see Elaine.

6

While I traveled by train and bus to my mother's facility, a team entered the cabin of the airplane to clean it up before the next group of passengers boarded. I had used a cup, and a wrapper for the peanuts, and a napkin. I had missed the trash collection round by the flight attendant, absorbed in my puzzle, so had left them all stuffed in the seat pocket, where a person was now reaching in and adding them to a larger trash bag full of similar items. I thought of those things, too, as I rode to see my mother, as I often did. Little droppings of my existence.

7

Over the years, my mother had become a beloved resident; she was charming, and easy to be with, and skillful at coaxing people from sedentary spaces to gather together for evening activities. She could also sing at a piano, and there was a dingy brown one with tobacco-stained keys just like a person's teeth wedged in the main room's corner. No one knew where the piano had come from; its tone was resonant and full, but the high D was broken, and she would supply the real high D when the tall older man with the cracked knuckles would sit on the bench and play Christmas carols at any time of year. This room was usually where my aunt and I found her at our visits, and that particular one, as I walked toward the main living room area by myself, heart tripping, palms damp, passing the open window screens that let in the perfume of squashed summer fruits and flowers, the fecund abundance of August in northern Oregon, that was exactly what she was doing.

She sat close to the piano player on the wooden bench, a colorful scarf wrapped around her shoulders, her auburn hair combed and thickly wavy. He was finishing up "Sleigh Bells," and as I quietly approached the room, they started in on the opening notes of "My Funny Valentine," which had always been one of her favorites. What a wash of sensation I found in those notes, in a song she had sometimes murmured to me at bedtime. The pianist played with confidence, clearly someone who had been accompanying singers all his life, and though I had seen him many times before, I still did not know if he was a resident, or a visitor, or staff. My mother's throaty alto took ahold of the song, and once I reached the edge of the doorway, I stopped, leaning as softly as I could against the wall to listen, far enough back so that I would not yet influence the room.

I knew this room very well. I took first some orientation just by being at the edge of it. It was a shabby room but pretty, lined with old books and vintage furniture, and decorated with faded paintings in ornate golden frames of cliffside seascapes that had all been donated by a resident's wealthy relative. It had always been my favorite location of the visit. Most of the other residents were in the next room over, sitting in front of the TV, or settled on the rusting loveseats inside the atrium in the middle of the building, heads tilted back to look at an exposed square of sky, but those rooms had always seemed haphazard to me, thrown together without purpose, whereas the shabby room itself had the aura of a decaying European castle, and before I announced my presence to my person of significance inside it, I let its familiarity and broken elegance pour over me. Those paintings had been anchors for me during so many visits before; I doubted any other visitor knew so well the details of those beach scenes and their pails and wave crests and gradations of sunset. Or, perhaps they did. Perhaps many of us, resident and visitor alike, had learned those beach scenes to their core.

"Don't change a hair for me," sang my mother, with feeling. The music climbed the scale, and the piano made its thudding plunk for the high D, and her voice supplied a perfectly pitched ringing D against it, and the dissonance between the two seemed a helpful analogy for her state of being, one that seemed to meld and rotate between the broken D and the whole D, forever and ever amen.

She hadn't seen me yet, but across the room, a nurse working on paperwork at a chipped, engraved teak desk glanced up and gave me a nod.

At some point I must've changed my position in the doorframe; the wood creaked and my mother whipped around, crying out, and then ran over to hug me, grasping my shoulders. "How long have you been there?" she asked, her eyes shining with tears. "You made it!" After thanking the pianist, who smiled at her, she pulled me to the side like we were guests at a party, bringing me over to the usual tattered green silk chairs; "Come," she said, holding my hand in hers, "sit, tell me everything. How was the flight? How was it by yourself?" I gave her the biscotti, and she laughed, peering in the bag. "My sister," she said, shaking her head. "Thinking of everything."

It was awkward without my aunt there; we bumped around our sentences as if we'd just met, and when my mother asked again about the flight I told her every detail I could think of, hanging on to the tiny pieces of information like they were stepping-stones between us, which they were, including telling her my drink choice, and information about my seat companion, and how long I had waited for the bus (twenty minutes) while she listened with her large and hungry eyes. At some point her gaze began to move around my face, and she reached out her arms and held me back by the shoulders to look at me more directly. "Aren't you such a gorgeous young woman?" she said, grasping my arms. "Look at you! Seventeen!"

"Seventeen."

She complimented my hair, which was in a regular ponytail, and my clothes, which were the navy blue version of the sweatpants and sweatshirts that were my latest response to the pressures of adolescence. It was like she was complimenting the barest fact of my being. I was not a gorgeous teen; gorgeous was not ever the right word for me, but I knew, could feel, the bright light I was bringing her by sitting there.

She wiped her eyes with a tissue. Our last visit had been almost eight months ago. She looked older in the summer sun, the lines around her eyes finer, more plentiful.

My mother told me again how there was a space for me at lunch right next to her, right at her table, and that the food was decent because there was a new cook, a talented woman named Lucy, who maybe we could meet when the meal was over. She talked about her daily routine, how she had been singing all the time, and had started helping with the arrangement of a nightly entertainment schedule, which made her feel more useful, which she appreciated. She talked of her talented friend Edward, who had grown up in the south of India, and who still had lots of family there, and who could sing when no one was listening with a soulful vibrato, which she tried to demonstrate with a heartiness that mortified my teenage self even though no one except the working nurse was in the room. "Edward is the piano player," she added, nodding at the piano though he had left. She asked more about me, and I spoke first of Vicky, who had developed an interest in the school musical, and had been, at nine years old, a successful helping hand to her teacher in the wings for their production of **You're a Good Man, Charlie Brown,** and about how Uncle Stan had gotten a new crew job with an action film that might even end up as a series, and how Aunt Minn was working with a new employee at the middle school office who was giving her a hard time by being late every morning. I spoke about my classes, particularly how much I'd liked frog dissection in biology, and how I was starting to collect items from yard sales to resell when I happened to pass by, which I really enjoyed, and maybe was even a little good at, and about my friend Deena, who wore these tiny white faux-leather outfits all the time and who said she preferred my company over any other because I never overshadowed her. My mother made responsive sounds at appropriate times, huhs and aahs, wincing at the Deena statement, making sure to tell me that my appeal was understated but still beautiful, and how she didn't want anyone to diminish me, and that she thought I would definitely pick objects very well; I explained how it really was a good deal for both me and for Deena, because Deena liked the spotlight, and I did not, and the words moved back and forth between us like some kind of rubber band, a way to keep us linked to one another while we got used to the feeling of being just the two of us together, but it was prelude and overture anyway, because all the while as we spoke, and as I did the filling in, getting the updates out of the way like they were bushes to clear on a trail hike, as the cliffside landscapes around us crashed painterly steel-colored waves onto those pointillated sandy beaches, I could feel, like a hard thing forming within me, what I really wanted to bring up now that I had her alone.

"Mom," I said. I ran my fingertips over the fraying cloth of the chair seat, where the wood below began to curl into plumes. "There is something I wanted to talk to you about."

"Anything," my mother said, taking my hand. "Please, honey. Nothing would make me happier."

"It is going to sound strange."

"I'm all about the strangeness," she said, bobbing her head. "You know that."

"But I think my mind is okay," I said.

Her eyes were so intent on mine, so glued. "Listen, Francie. Listen. You are the most stable person I know. You don't have what I have. Mine was a problem at birth, my mother talked about it from birth! You know they bumped me on the table, right? You were such a capable baby. You crawled at seven months old. It was amazing. I'm sure you're okay."

Then I lost my nerve. I made up some story about a guy I liked at school, in a nonexistent chem class, basing him on the man whom I talked with sometimes at the local library who was at least ten years older, likely gay, and had a way of crunching the hair on his head while searching for books that I found appealing. She went on for twenty minutes about birth control, and once back in Burbank, I received several letters in envelopes half-licked containing stuffed pages of articles about different brands of condoms, miraculously delivered by the mail carrier. We veered in the conversation and talked more about Edward, and the entertainment schedule, and when a breeze swelled through the window screen, she pulled her scarf more closely around her shoulders, a giant paisley patterned piece of cloth she said she'd gotten as a gift from Aunt Minn. "Will you take a photo to show her?" she asked, and we asked the nurse, who took many: of her, of me, of her and me, of both of us wrapped in the scarf together, and when we were done and back in the same green silk chairs, and I perceived another opening in the conversation, I tried again.

"When you smashed your hand," I said, squeezing her good one, beneath the oil-shaped cliffs, to the sound of silverware clattering and the wheeling of the table-setting cart as the staff prepared lunch in the dining area, "I went to stay two nights with the babysitter before I took the train to Aunt Minnie and Uncle Stan's."

"God bless that babysitter," my mother said. "She saved me. I was barely able to think then, Francie. Did you know? I was tied to the bed. All I did was yell about seeing you."

"And she had a lamp in her living room," I said. "Of butterflies."

"How lovely," my mother said, nodding and nodding. Her eyes were damp, and she seemed to want to affirm everything before it even left my mouth. "I always loved her jewelry. She seemed very thoughtful with her selections."

"On the morning I was leaving, I saw something."

"Okay."

"It was a butterfly," I said.

"Yes," she said, pressing my hand. "How pretty that sounds. A lamp of butterflies."

"Except this was a real butterfly," I said. "It had fallen into a glass of water."

Her eyes, still so focused on mine. In the background, the same man with the knuckles and vibrato, Edward, had returned to the piano to play some light medleys, and I vaguely recognized a classic rock song about taking off a load. There was some stirring outside the living room area as residents rose from their seats to walk to the dining room, toward the growing aroma of what smelled like chili. My mother was blinking at me, with her warm doggish eyes, and broken lashes, one bent and high on her cheek, her coarse and generous beauty, and her throat rose and fell with a swallow and I could see, suddenly, obviously, how wrong it was to tell her. I had, for years, taken that care to avoid telling Aunt Minn anything about the butterfly, or the beetle, not wanting to burden her, or frighten her, but wasn't it far worse to choose the person whose lines between mind and world were already frail?

"How sad," my mother said.

"Yes," I said. "It was dead."

"How sad," she said again, and her gaze began to scatter.

"It was the same color and pattern as the ones on the lampshade," I said, pushing on anyway. "And, it was floating in the water, directly below the lampshade."

"My goodness."

"And the babysitter's windows were closed."

"What a clever butterfly, wasn't it, to find a small space to fly in."

"I did not see any small spaces."

"Portland is known for its butterflies."

"The coloring was just like the ones on the lamp," I said. "Exactly."

"There were real butterflies on the lamp?"

"No. There were pictures of butterflies on the lamp."

"It was a picture floating in the water?"

"No. It was a real butterfly floating in the water glass."

She tugged at the scarf to wrap it around herself more tightly. It was really an enormous scarf, nearly the size of a twin bedsheet. I had no idea where my aunt had found it.

"What a very odd coincidence," she said, brightly. "What did the babysitter say?"

"I didn't show her."

She shifted in her chair.

"Why not then? Why not show her?"

"I don't know," I said.

"Did you take a picture?"

"No."

"Do you have it here?"

"I drank it," I said.

"This was how many years ago? You didn't show Shrina?"

"No," I said. "I swallowed it down with the glass of water, and then she took me to the train."

"Who else did you tell?"

"You are the first person I'm telling."

It was like lightly unhooking a necklace, the one that held her thinking together. I couldn't seem to stop myself. And she wasn't the first I had told, not at all; I had told Vicky the whole story of spotting and drinking the butterfly in the water glass many, many times over. I had shown Vicky the beetle from my purple knapsack when she was four years old, in a beam of sunlight in her room, like a talisman dredged from the river of a dreamworld. Months before this visit, I had even told a random and handsome young man at a long bus stop wait one afternoon about how that same dead beetle had first been on a paper, and then had rested on my palms on the train, telling the story slowly, in a spooky voice, before we headed over the hill into Hollywood to attend a Halloween parade. He had listened with focused eyes, tilting in, tapping his knee, and had he not terrified me with his attentiveness, I might have walked to the parade alongside, and told him more. But for whatever reason, that day, I wanted to amplify a pressure on my mother, and I wanted her to think it was all hers, and as soon as I had her alone I couldn't help myself. I paused in my chair. The storm clouds in the painting glowed with a steely intensity. My mother pulled the scarf around her body even tighter, as she had done with the excess crocheted July blankets years earlier, always wrapping herself in things, swaddling herself, and then, as she waited for me to continue, she somehow began inching her wrapped tight body up the high back of the green chair.

"I'm sorry to bother you," I said. "Maybe I shouldn't have said anything—"

"Of course you should tell me," my mother said, rising up the back of the chair.

"Mom?" I said.

"I'm honored," she said, edging her body higher as if it was the only possible exit from the conversation.

"Are you okay? Nurse?" I said.

"I—" my mother said.

"Nurse!" I said, and my mother bent herself over the back of the chair and tipped her whole body over. She fell to the floor and banged her shoulder and the side of her head as I rushed around, and the nurse across the room who was still doing paperwork at the same teak desk ran over. We helped my mother up and she wasn't bleeding, just dazed, a little shaken, and when the nurse asked what happened, what was wrong, my mother said nothing, nothing, but her hands now emerging from the wrap of the scarf were beginning to spring around in that rabbity way I knew so well but hadn't seen in years. "Stay back," the nurse told me, harsh, and she helped my mother to her feet and let my mother lean hard on her arm and led her to the room she shared with someone else, someone powerfully old, so faded and bony she barely registered in the blankets. I asked if I should still stay for lunch, if my mother was going to be able to have lunch, or what I should do, and the nurse shook her head, not looking at me, mumbling something to the floor, about how lunch wasn't going to happen; she asked me not to go too close to say goodbye, but just to wave from the doorway supervised as my mother lay tucked in bed with her hair spread over the pillow like a child from another century. My mother had a glass of water at her bedside with a pill bottle, a framed school photo of me, and a classic lampshade of pure white, and I—waving from the doorway, shaking with guilt and meanness and now a desperate desire to leave, still felt a great pitch of relief that the only thing that could fall into her water off her lampshade would be white light, the emptiness of white light. "I'm so sorry," I told a different nurse, who walked me past the dining hall with its clinking of forks and light chatter, out to the front of the facility where she stood with me on the brick steps looking at the full speckled world, humid and touched with purple and orange, bounty from the months of rain. "She'll be okay," said the nurse, "we'll take good care of her. When's your flight?" "Not for four hours," I said. "I—" "Honey," said the nurse, gently, patting my shoulder, "go early."

8

I think of this now from the balcony of my apartment in the depths of the San Fernando Valley, where I live on the third floor of a sand-colored stucco building about a ten-minute bus ride from my aunt and uncle's home. I have lived here, in this particular apartment, for three years, and have stayed in Los Angeles for nearly twenty.

One afternoon many months ago, on a day of nothing notable except a certain familiar emptiness rolling out at its edges inside me, after walking home at dusk from my managerial job at the framing store down the street which I had taken because it was maybe of interest to me, business, although I disliked the place and the hours and the act of constant framing, I'd settled on the balcony, eating a bag of potato chips, gazing at a couple of leafy orange trees, remnants of a bygone grove. For whatever reason, something was unusually quiet inside me that day, looking out, as if some new space had opened up for a moment, like a rotating door revealing its slim aperture of access to the outside, and through this opening an image had slid into my head steady and true of what it had been like on the playground in Portland, at Lewis and Clark Elementary, those many years ago. There I was, eight years old, standing by myself in the middle of the playground, totally still with the windy air, the diamond-patterned fence, the melting cracker taste in my mouth. Tracking. How the other kids running around thought I was still frozen from some long-past game of tag, and on the way back to class, had swatted my shoulder to unfreeze me.

From the balcony, I could see someone walk out of a store, and someone walk into a store, and cars pulling away from the metered curb, and new cars gliding into place. My apartment was near the corner, so my scope of view included pedestrians stepping into their cars on Chandler, and a glimpse of Victory Boulevard and all the commercial activity there. It was a cloudy afternoon in July, and the blasting heat of summer had not yet fully baked the valley into brown, so the hills still showed swaths of rolling green patched with bands of blazing yellow. I ate my bag of potato chips and sat next to the small succulent plant in its terracotta pot left behind by a previous tenant, and for a moment felt myself living inside both times at once. Why had the memory risen up right then? I did not know.

It was, overall, a scattered time in my life. I was

twenty-six years old. I went to my framing job nearly every day and stood behind the counter and took orders and offered opinions on metal versus wood. I filled up my Friday and Saturday nights with activities initiated by others. I attended a few dinners in which I and another person eyed each other as potential mates, after a recent breakup with a fellow whom my aunt and Vicky had asked about almost constantly with delighted winks in their voices, but other than my continued weekend outings to yard sales to hunt for items to sell online, it all felt like further performances of participation, just as I had experienced in the third-grade classroom, sitting at a table and talking and joking with the other students as if I were there. I inhabited none of it, and the sensation I was recalling right then on the balcony, the memory of standing still and paying attention until that hand arrived on my shoulder, of the girl calling, "Francie's frozen again!" and all the kids laughing—this memory evoked something different, something else, like catching a whiff of a fragrant long-ago scent from a far-off and regal country. I hadn't even minded being teased about standing so still like a lump; it had been sweet, the teasing. It had never stopped me.

On the balcony, a breeze blew over my face, and cars stopped at the red light, and then moved forward at the green light, and the memory of the playground began to slip, the hand releasing my shoulder, freeze tag over, body disappearing into time.

Then I went inside, and threw out the potato chip bag, and made some plans for the weekend, and forgot again.

9

The next thing that happened, a few days later, was an almost overwhelming desire to rearrange the items on my balcony, and build myself a tent.

It hadn't started as an idea about a tent; I'd had the thought about the playground while on the balcony, and although the details of it didn't fully stick, something of its impression remained, of a different kind of pace, and with that, I canceled a few of my nighttime plans, seeing how it felt to let the evenings unfurl, time rushing into the corners. From my apartment, I could hear that traffic rushing along on Victory and cars driving to and fro on Chandler as I sat in my living room, and as a kind of vague tribute to that younger self, without planning what I was doing, closed my eyes and tried to listen to the cars, to feel my feet on the carpet. To smell, and cough from, the faint sprinkling of dust from the ceiling fan whirring above. I wasn't entirely sure what I was doing, and when I opened my eyes the walls seemed far away, almost impossibly far, stretching beyond me, and the lines around myself looser, in a bad way, not like it had been on the playground at all. I stood and began to move around the apartment, sorting through the mail. I did not, I thought, tossing ads, opening bills, affixing stamps, piling catalogues, belong so well to the middles of rooms. I snacked on some tortilla chips. I cleaned the tub.

Still, something seemed to be shifting, bubbling beneath, and as I went about my daily routines, memories of that transition in my life, the time from when my mother smashed her hand until I arrived at the doorstep in Burbank, California, were seeming to hover near me, operating as a kind of shimmering peripheral haze. I could feel the memories there, wanting my attention, but I did not know what to do with them. I considered calling up my mother to talk to her about what she recalled of that particular time, but it certainly hadn't worked well before, and she'd already been having a rough week; at our weekly Sunday phone call it had been hard to understand her, her words scrambled, sentences in code. This happened sometimes, had its own kind of rhythm, and Aunt Minn had been talking extensively with the doctors, and my mother was trying another new medication, and the last thing she needed, truly the last-last thing, was a call from her daughter wanting details about her hospital visit almost twenty years ago while I went on again about butterflies dropping from lampshades. I attended my yard sales. I canceled more plans. I told Vicky on the phone that she was always welcome to come over, but that she would be the main exception because something in my schedule, or my daily structure, was changing, though I could not fully pinpoint what; "a kind of going under," I said, flicking rubber bands against the kitchen counter, so many rubber bands from the grocery store, in a little red and green pile. Vicky was tapping away on her computer as we talked, and said fine, and that she was used to me doing curious and inexplicable things anyway, and then informed me that two of the boys in her senior class had literally grown a head taller over the past month of summer when she saw them recently at a party. "Science fiction," she said, chewing on something. "Happening right here." She asked if I could help her with her college essay, which I said I'd be glad to do, which was true, and when we hung up, in addition to everything else, the specter of her college departure now hung over the rooms. She would be leaving in about a year. She would likely choose to live somewhere else. I had been in one family shape that had gone through dramatic change so long ago, and I knew the feel of it, could smell the transition, cucumber and trash, from a far distance.

That evening, with nothing left to do, and all my packaging tasks completed, I went online and looked up all the yard sales I could find for the next couple of weeks, cross-checking with the Metro site, figuring out the ones closest to easily accessible bus routes to see if by attending more I could make enough money to quit the framing job and do object sales full-time. With Vicky's help, earlier in the year I'd opened a shop online, where I uploaded the photos of all I'd found at the yard sales, and the store itself was doing surprisingly well—I had a number of designated shoppers who checked inventory regularly, and a high star count. The month previous, I'd been able to cover my rent and most of my food and utility bills with the profits. For whatever reason, I seemed to have a modest talent for selecting objects from piles of clutter that, once cleaned, other people might want to buy more than all the other objects speckling the world, competing for their wallets. I scheduled my weekend accordingly: four sales on Saturday, three on Sunday that I could fit in before the weekly dinner at my aunt and uncle's home after which we would speak to my mother again and see how she was doing. I looked out the window. In the evening lamplight, a neighbor across the street was hauling a box from a furniture store out of the trunk of her car and into her home. She had family members lugging additional boxes with her. It was a thing of many parts. A bed frame? A dresser? Regardless, it meant something else, some reject, might be on her curb soon. I would surely keep an eye out.

All was in reach. If I was willing to drop the

framing job, if I was willing to unframe everything else with it, including the regular schedule of my nine-to-five days, then something else—I did not know what—might happen.

During the daytime, while I considered all these possibilities, I walked to my job, which was located twelve blocks away in a strip mall on Victory, sharing space with a bagel shop, a taqueria, and a box/mailing store that I thought was wildly overpriced. I had been working at the framing store for almost a year, and there, I assisted customers with all their framing needs, on this day writing up the measurements and notes for, in part, the mounting of a desertscape, a family collage of photographs, and a vintage movie noir poster of a woman in vinyl boots holding a whip. A woman in a cargo vest brought in a purple watercolor squiggle her three-year-old had made that she said, laughing, she wanted forever. An expressionless man presented to me the cardstock Italian food menu we all got on our doorknobs every day and insisted he wanted it framed, soon, please, in oak. Was it his restaurant? I asked, writing down the notes. No, he said, unoffering. I brought the stacks of order forms to Edwin, who did all the framing work in the back, and then returned to my counter. The day was feeling long, longer than usual. The summer sun filled the windows and turned them white with light, and the radio playlist circled through the same batch of songs, soggy with pep, and my boss came and went with her clicky open-backed heels, waggling fingers at me as I sat on my stool.

During the slowest hours, I scrolled around on my phone underneath the ledge, but I was finding myself newly uninterested in replying to the different messages and few invitations coming my way from people I did not really know very well. A friend from college invited me to a beach gathering, and I told her thank you but I was going out of town for a little while, and when she said where? how fun! I just said Portland, which was not true, and left it at that. In a way, it was true, in another way, in another sort of travel modality, as I'd been thinking of my mother all week as she tried out this new medication, me imagining her in her room, or at the piano, or sitting in one of those lime green silk chairs, staring out the window at the feathery ferns of the city. I organized the rows of frame corners yet again. I ate my lunch at the worktable in the back room. This new medication, according to my aunt, had done well in its most recent trials, and had minimal side effects compared to some of the others, so as I finished my sandwich and chewed up my apple slices, I wondered about how she might be when we spoke to her on the phone on Sunday after our meal, and I also thought about the nature of politeness, as I'd just experienced with the beach party gathering exchange, and how you had to tell a person just enough information to get them to stop asking. What a delicate balance it all was. I was feeling relieved, bundling up my paper bag and tossing it into the trash, washing my hands in the sink, clearing apple peel from my teeth, because the Portland statement about the beach party gathering had been the right calibration. The friend had sent me a smiley face emoji, and with that, the encounter was done, nothing dangling.

That same afternoon, when I was back at my counter, eyes heavy with after-lunch sleepiness and boredom, daring myself not to look at the clock, a woman came into the store to the tinkling of the entrance bell and walked right up to my desk. She was wearing large red hoops in her ears and was carrying a crumpled paper bag that looked a lot like the lunch bag I'd just thrown into the trash in the back room. She shook it out, and a beetle tumbled onto the black cloth display square at the front of the counter. It was a beautiful sharkskin green scarab June beetle, small, with gleaming wings, and a geometric body. She told me she had found it, dead, on her travels to Spain, just lying on the sidewalk like an abandoned jewel. It had been in this bag in her to-do pile for years, and she couldn't believe she was actually here getting around to it. "Stunning, isn't it?" she said, as I lifted it with silver tongs and we looked at it together on a square of white muslin. The memory I had of my beetle, the stag beetle I had first seen illustrated on a test, and then held in my palms in my sleeper car, and which

I had dropped, years later, onto a bus, rose with a flash of intensity, though this particular memory did not emerge in any kind of full form—it came to me in parts, in fragments and pieces, tugging at the corners of my thinking like a half-captured dream. "Wood?" asked the woman, peering at the rows of decorative right angles chevroning the walls, "Or maybe silver?" I pulled down a thin gilded frame, which contrasted so well with the shimmering green, and we matched it to the corners until we found the best width, and the woman smiled happily as I added it to the work pile. "I will cherish it," she said warmly. She thanked me twice and went to pay, but it all still felt like such a show to me; one of the reasons I didn't like my framing job was because at the yard sales I came across so many of these framed items dusty on tables, piled in stacks, long forgotten. It was hard to imagine this bug doing anything but disappearing into its wall. My shift was up, and I waved goodbye to my boss over at her side desk, talking on her phone, and went to get my backpack from the back room, which now smelled strongly of peanut butter. Plus, I thought, shouldering the backpack, it was just unnerving to think of this bug soon under glass, when it had once been crawling on the ground doing its bug life in Barcelona. As I turned the corner and began to walk home down Victory, a necklace of red and white tract housing looping through the soft curves of the Verdugo hills, a squirrel darting across the sidewalk dragging a half-eaten fig, it did strike me how opposite it was from the dead butterfly that had emerged from the lampshade at the babysitter's apartment, or the dead beetle that had exited the paper on the train, or the dried roses, so many years later, that had dropped from the curtains at Deena's. Three visitations. Three events. I passed the homeless man with his painting display of still lifes, and the dancing person wearing a giant arrow suit, pointing to the television and video game console store across the street. I had not spent much time thinking about these episodes since that terrible visit to my mother's facility ten years back, when I had sent her over the back of a chair, but as I pressed the button for the crosswalk, I thought, for a moment, for the length of the red flashing hand, that it might be worth my own time, through some other way, to consider them again.

The light changed, and I moved myself between the yellow lines, past the row of humming car grilles, past the pool supply store and foam mart, thinking about the shop, and how I might improve my speed of delivery, and admiring in my mind the new pale green ceramic sugar jar and creamer I'd found that weekend at a yard sale in Sherman Oaks, and what sort of background might best showcase their most delicate porcelain beauty.

10

"Come," said my uncle. "Come sit on the steps and wait with me. We have a little time," looking at his watch, "before she can come out and get you. Do you want a mint? Have you ever been to her apartment? I've always preferred the train myself, to tell you the truth. I took it to New York City from Baltimore all the time. There'll be a dining car, I'm sure. Big windows. Ocean view."

He picked up a stick and drew a line in the dirt at the side of the steps. "You're here now . . ." he said, pointing at a pebble nestled in the grass, and then dragged the stick down the dirt at a rough angle that slightly resembled the coasts of Oregon and California until it rested at the foot of the steps, ". . . to here." He picked up another pebble and placed it at the end of the stick. We looked at the pathway together, from one pebble to another.

Then he hopped the stick eastward and poked a gray gum blob on the walkway. "And, Vegas!" he said, laughing, before he pulled out his phone to begin making calls.

11

The tent itself came into being due to some comments initially from Vicky. On Sunday, a few days after the sighting of the scarab beetle at the framing store, I took the bus down Magnolia as I usually did to my aunt and uncle's home for our weekly dinner together. This had been a standing date on the calendar since I'd moved out of their house for college and beyond, and always included that call to my mother after the meal to check in. Her sentence wandering during the last week's phone call had led to my aunt paging the facility psychiatrist, which was the usual routine; it was always my aunt who took on this task. Their parents had died years before, but even when alive, they had not ever taken charge of their eldest daughter's care with my aunt's level of detail and rigor. She had a small coral pink notebook on her desk with lists of medication names and amounts, and a series of files marked **E** on her computer. Doctor numbers on her phone. New doctors listed after the old doctors left.

Printed articles about new treatments on tables and countertops, with bolded, underlined sentences to ask about on her next call.

She'd been on hold at Hawthorne House for a while last week, so I'd gone home while she was still waiting on the phone, and Vicky had reported to me that when she had finally completed the call, the medication had been changed, and my aunt retreated to the sofa in the living room with a glass of wine that remained undrunk, just staring at the off TV, breathing, unmoving, as we'd seen her do after similar interventions so many times before. The sense I always had of her in those times was of a person allowing a stress to physically pass through her. We knew not to talk to her. The wine was a prop that made it all look more presentable. Uncle Stan, also according to Vicky, had come home late from his job on the crew of the second sequel of the action film series that had been financially stabilizing for years but that was currently in production and taking up a lot of his extra time, and when he saw my aunt there, he quietly undid the dishwasher, and then went upstairs to talk to Vicky about a pool party that had been a source of familial war all week long.

That afternoon, I entered the house, and after I greeted my aunt and hugged and thanked her, giving her the carton of blueberries she'd requested, while she chopped up zucchini and onions to the sounds of news radio and waved me and my offer to help away, I went up the stairs to Vicky's bedroom, past the Vermont lamb/goat drawings, and the small framed sketches of jumping figures that my mother had drawn many years ago in an art therapy class in which the teacher had praised her sense of joy. Someone—most likely my aunt—had recently vacuumed, and on the stairs and at the landing, slanted sections of carpet showed areas of darkening purple, then lighter, then darker, in parallelograms of carpet fiber. Somewhere across the house, a vacuum bag rested beneath a plastic handle, puffed with the tiny bits of their lives, fingernails, dust, pretzel crumbs, hair.

Vicky, at that point, was soon to start twelfth grade. Already she was busy preparing for the school fall play, as lead lighting designer, and also making a list of schools to apply to, all of which had strong theater departments, though she had explained to me that she was not sure if she would rather do lighting design, or act, or write plays, or possibly stage-manage, or maybe direct. Any of the above, she'd told me. All of the above. The college application process was already stressful, and earlier in the week, she had sent me the three latest possibilities for her essay—one about her love of theater, another about her brief and frustrating interlude with soccer, and the third, her favorite, the one that her English teacher had liked best. I liked it too. It was a good essay. It was about her sister, who was really her cousin, who joined the family at the age of eight due to a spike in her mother's mental illness, and how she had made the family more interesting, and provided Vicky with true inspiration in her life.

"Come in!" Vicky called when she heard my footsteps on the stairs.

For a moment, I hovered at the landing. After I'd moved out, my bedroom, next to hers, had swiftly reverted to its role as half-office/exercise space, and I took a step closer and peeked inside. The bed was still in there, covered now with piles of books and clothing, and the printer began whirring from its new spot on the desk where I'd never done any of my homework, preferring always to work in Vicky's room instead. The old painted rainbow/cloud on the wall was now covered by the return of the rolled yoga mats and a secondhand standing bicycle I'd bought for my aunt a few years back at a sale in Van Nuys which she seemed to pedal happily on the rare rainy days.

I found Vicky cross-legged on her bed with her laptop open. "Printing a new copy for you right now," she said, glancing up. "I just looked at your site. It looks really good. Are those new bracelets?"

She darted up to grab the pages. I went to her computer to scroll through the site, to see how it looked on her screen, and when she came back told her how I'd found the bracelets dust-encrusted, in a jangle of jewelry in a pile just down the block at a surprise sale, not even really planning to look. They'd been a dollar apiece, and I was selling them, clean and sparkly, for twenty each now. One already had been bought by a woman in the Florida Keys.

Vicky listened carefully, with her gold-colored eyes, as she usually did. A ponytail sprouted from the top of her head.

"Two thousand percent markup," she said. "Not bad. Is it true you're going to quit your job?"

"I think so. I think I'm making enough."

"Amazing," she said. I had already settled into my usual spot at the end of her bed, and she sat down next to me, hitting her foot against mine. "You'd be your own boss," she said.

"Exactly. Aunt Minn thinks it might be a bit rash—"

"She thinks everything is rash. You should totally do it."

We sat facing her door, with the edges of all her old door stickers visible, just the white sticker back left, pictures gone. It was like she was already leaving, had already left. In a year, I'd be showing up to Sunday dinners with my aunt and uncle and sitting across the table from them, alone.

"Essay?" I said.

Vicky handed over the printed pages and pulled up the file on her computer.

"Knock yourself out," she said, tossing over a pen.

We sat side by side, working. I read quietly and circled some words, and she tapped around on her laptop. When I was ready, we went through the essay twice together, her reading parts aloud, us reordering a paragraph together and strengthening some of the word choices. At a natural pause, she opened a spreadsheet to show me where she was planning to apply; she'd made a careful list, with each college and its requirements and deadlines and the things she liked best about what she'd read or seen. These were schools located all around the country, none in Los Angeles, as I'd suspected: New York, New Haven, San Diego, Berkeley, Austin, Michigan, more. She highlighted one of the lines and quickly typed in some information she'd learned about financial aid. Below us, the salty smell of baking cheese drifted up from downstairs.

"Do you remember the story of the butterfly?" I asked, watching her letters fill the open slots.

"Of course," she said.

"I've been thinking about it a lot this week."

"Which part?"

"All the parts. And some other parts."

"Anything new?"

"It's just been bubbling up," I said. "The beetle too. I'm not sure why."

Her eyes blinked at me, the way they did sometimes, friendly but also tunneling in, ready to bulldoze me with devotion, and to my relief, Aunt Minn called us down to set the table. "I'm so glad you're here," Vicky said, in a low voice, as we tripped down the stairs. "It's been extra rough with her with Dad out so much and this party coming up. All week long. I think it's getting worse." "It?" "She. I don't know. You know what I mean." She went to gather forks and spoons from the silverware drawer, while I folded paper towels into napkins. Aunt Minn, lips pursed as if already trying to hold words inside herself, brought in the zucchini casserole between hands padded by oven mitts, and after I lit the tall candle in its silver boat, the three of us sat down to dinner. Uncle Stan was working overtime for at least two more weeks.

Aunt Minn and Vicky spoke in clipped tones, pass the zucchini, please, pass the rice, please, thank you, the hostility peppered with courtesy like balloons tied to lead weights, and as we ate, to offer some relief, I told a few stories about the yard sales I'd recently visited, including the man who'd tried to sell all his old mix tapes for two dollars apiece, and the woman in Alhambra who had probably a hundred different tangled extension and USB cords spilling from a gigantic box. They both listened closely. It seemed to be helping ease the tension at the table, and my aunt smiled with warmth in her eyes, eating slowly, which was a good sign because sometimes when worried she forgot to eat at all, so I kept going and started talking next about the babysitter's porcelain soap dish, and how I'd just had a thought the other day about how it had been shaped like a little dinghy, and how lovely it had been, with its graceful bar of lavender soap inside. "She had such a beautiful apartment," I said. "It was like a fairyland to me." "Did you ever visit her, after you moved?" Vicky asked, and I said no, though she'd sent me a few cards here and there. "Sometimes a birthday card," I said. "I think." The two of them kept their eyes pinned on me. Vicky spoke about lavender, and why it was her favorite smell, and my aunt joined in and said she also very much liked lavender, and then Vicky said she thought maybe she preferred rosemary, and I laughed a little at both of them, and then Vicky said, circling a long string of cheese around her fork, that it was true that whenever I talked about my Portland memories, they did have this sticky, three-dimensional quality to her, like they could be washed off, or picked at.

"I don't know how to describe it, but I just remember those things you say differently than other things," she said, waving her fork. "Like, it makes me feel like I have to wash my hands. But not in a bad way."

"Of course not," I said, "in that great sticky hands kind of way."

Aunt Minn laughed softly, pressing her fork tines sideways into her zucchini slice until the cooked flesh split through the metal.

"You two," she said.

We talked for a while about soap dishes, and how maybe I should have a designated part of my shop only for unique soap dishes, and both of them were so enthusiastic about the topic that it was obviously only there to block further discussion of Sammy's pool party the next weekend. Sammy's parents were never around and Sammy had once come to school drunk and Aunt Minn wanted assurance, possibly in writing, that Vicky would not drink or do drugs while she was there, which Vicky found too formal and not necessary and said she really was only interested in swimming, anyway, and maybe hanging out with a guy from her history class. This I had been hearing about from both sides all week long. Aunt Minn wanted to be sure Vicky knew very clearly about the family's history of psychotic breaks, and her own risk factors, and Vicky said the main risk factor in her life was the act of being bathed in constant anxiety, and they had said this to each other in new and varied ways all the time, like an overplayed duet on the radio. At the end of the meal, Aunt Minn went to the kitchen to bring in the bowl of fruit, and Vicky, eager to change the subject, grabbed her phone to see if there was any existing soap dish store, expertly searching and tapping and enlarging, finally showing us photos of a few boat-shaped versions, and another inexplicably shaped like a rat.

When the meal was over, and only leftover grains of rice and single stray blueberries remained on the table, Aunt Minn returned to the kitchen and brought the landline phone to the table. The three of us formed a triangle around it, leaning in, and the nurse connected us to my mother's room. This was the first time I'd spoken to my mother since the week before, when she'd been so hard to understand, her words upside down, inside out. "Hello?" she said, once it connected, and Aunt Minn and Vicky piped in right away with their greetings, "Hello, Aunt E!" "Hi, Elaine," "What's going on in Portland?" "What's the weather like there?" "Hi, Mom," I said, after a pause, and she let out a wave of glad sounds. "Francie," she said, "Minnie. Vicky. I'm so happy to hear you all."

It was immediately clear that she was better. Her voice had firmed back up. Her fluctuations of tones matched ours. Her sentences followed through. She asked how we were all doing, and Vicky jumped in, telling her about the upcoming fall play, and the blue tones she was hoping to use in the lighting scheme to fill the stage with a sense of mystery, and loss, which my mother listened to with interest, and Aunt Minn said something about how glad she was that Elaine was doing better, and that her shoulder was bothering her but on the whole she was doing fine, and I said how I'd made a big sale when I'd found a charming miniature grandfather clock in Atwater that had been broken but easy to fix. It was an exchange of health we were having, updates of functionality, and my mother responded to everyone with beautifully fitting noises of all kinds. When it was her turn, she told us about how her medication was much better, and she was feeling much more like herself again, and there was a job opening at the bakery down the street that she was considering applying for, and about how she was becoming closer with that friend Edward, the piano player of so many years with the strong lungs and the warm manner. Her voice sounded tinny and pleased through the phone lines. She asked what we'd had for dinner, which she always asked, and my aunt went through the menu, after which my mother told us that she and Edward had just read reviews online of a new restaurant in walking distance with an unusually special and reasonably priced eggplant dish that maybe sometime we could all try together. The three of us nodded; Aunt Minn clapped her hands. "Next visit!" my aunt said, "please." At some point, Vicky got up to wipe down the table, and I watched all the last pieces of rice and blueberries connect to her sponge and gather together to fall into her hand. When we said goodbye, my mother sent kisses through the phone, and Aunt Minn walked the handset back to the kitchen.

As we headed to the kitchen to wash dishes, I could feel inside me the snag of an unfinished thought, although I couldn't quite locate what it was. Vicky scraped the plates, and I rinsed, and Aunt Minn reordered the dishwasher to make space. It didn't seem to come from the phone call—that had gone smoothly, and had eased something in me, like always, hearing my mother's voice back to stable, and how the medications had kicked in. Although the illness could still swerve and jag inside her, the bounce-back was now notably faster and better. Vicky cleaned the serving plate with the small purple flowers that couldn't fit in the dishwasher, and I rubbed it dry with a dishtowel, and as we moved through the routine we'd been through after so many meals before, folding in Uncle Stan's parts, sweeping, neatening, all three of us talked about the latest news, including the disturbing sight of an influx of polar bears at certain villages in Russia, and a congressperson's new bill about health care, and then we went over the phone conversation with my mother together, safe territory, revisiting the high points like we'd all just seen the same movie: Edward, bakery, eggplant dish.

Once the floor was clean, and the dishwasher began its series of hummings, I hugged Aunt Minn and Vicky, leaving them to each other, while I carried the unfinished thought within me, and its tiny, almost negligible, itch. My bus ride home was a beautiful lit hallway, traveling the streets. Other buses crossed in the opposite direction, wheeled containers full of gleaming white light. Inside mine, the only other passengers were an older man, nodding off to sleep, and a younger woman in a jogging suit, tapping away at her phone. The traffic lights were mostly green. We passed a mirrored office building, in which I could see our bus, moving through the squares, and the three of us plus driver inside it, and the woman's focus on her phone reminded me of Vicky and her own looking up of the soap dishes, and right then the word **sticky** came back, and my thought returned to its track, a train lining up synaptically that I could now get on and ride. Sticky, I thought. It was the thing about the sticky memories. As we turned up Victory, I found, watching the man's nodding head as a rhythmic companion to my thinking, that I had wanted to reconsider what Vicky had said at the table with her fork waving in the air—something about the idea of formed memories, of treating the memories like something to capture. It seemed useful to me. I could make some use of that idea. Perhaps, I thought, as I got off the bus and walked to my apartment, the nighttime wide and starless above, the quiet and tucked-away quality of Sunday evening, up the stairs and past some of my neighbors' apartments, with the clinking of dishes in sinks, and the fading smell of fried meat, that was what I had been looking for.

12

The beetle had come, in its way, before the butterfly. I met it first on its piece of paper, on the lawn of the elementary school, as my uncle and I waited for the babysitter to finish up her end-of-the-week classroom preparations. Once she was done and came out to meet us, she would drive me to her apartment, and he could jump back into his red rental car and race to the airport to fly home and greet his infant daughter, who was, at that moment, getting ready to burrow through the birth canal. My aunt, hundreds of miles away, explaining to the obstetric nurse between contractions just why he couldn't be there yet. My mother massively sedated at a different hospital, in a different city, in a different wing. I remember it was a Friday, because everyone we spoke to said have a good weekend at the end of the exchange, like a kind of punctuation, and to keep us out of the way while we waited for the babysitter, my uncle had guided me to the concrete steps at the front of the school, offering me his tin of mints, drawing maps of the West in the dirt, both of us hunching in our sweaters and jackets while we waited for the older grades to get out. Or, while I waited for the older grades to get out, and he pulled out his phone again, making the series of calls to set up my care.

I didn't know my uncle all that well at that point, and this was my introduction to what I now would call his outrageous efficiency; within ten minutes, he had contacted the train reservation line and bought two tickets, and then through several other brisk and impenetrable conversations secured me a trusted steward, a second cousin on his side who lived in Seattle who could come down and ride with me from Portland's Union Station to the end stop in downtown Los Angeles, which was a good place to get off, easy and final, and where my uncle explained he himself would be picking me up in the main parking lot by the taxis on what would be Monday evening. "I will be the one in the Orioles cap," he said, tapping the brim of his Orioles cap. Trees rustled. The flag made whipping cloth sounds high on its pole. My uncle jotted down some notes on several slips of paper, with the babysitter's name on one of them, underlined, and explained to me that the babysitter would be introducing me to this steward/cousin at the train station on Sunday, and the steward would apparently be wearing a red zipper sweater with a train on it. "I haven't seen him in a few years, but he's extremely nice," said my uncle, folding the papers and tucking the slips into his jacket pocket, "very dependable, easy to be with." "Will he talk to me?" I asked. "If you don't want him to, then no." "I don't want him to." "I will pass that along." The lawn shone green, and the air chilled, and with each small action he took, I could feel the adults shuttling into a line, myself the red baton passed from runner to runner like I'd seen the previous year during the Olympics, which I had watched for hours with my mother because she could not stop staring at the primacy of a running body: "That's health right there," she'd said, fake-smoking a broken chopstick. My uncle had also called her hospital for an update, and found out she was a little better, but not in any way ready to talk on the phone.

The beetle, my future beetle, was not present in any of this. At that point, the beetle was just a drawing on a paper in someone else's backpack. It was being shoved in the backpack probably right around then. Getting zipped up, but with zipper not fully closed. The teacher was saying the last messages before the weekend at the front of a classroom to a room full of restlessness. The kid upon whose test lived the beetle was likely staring at the clock. Ready to go home. To have a weekend. To play some ball.

My uncle, done with his tasks, smiled at me, and then, with the slightest of movements, pivoted his body away and called up my aunt again in her hospital room. As soon as she picked up, his phone manner slowed and quieted, and he gathered the same crooked maple stick off the steps that he'd used earlier to draw my route, poking at more gum blobs on the concrete. He spoke very close into the phone, as if he was trying to mesh himself through it. "She seems okay," he said softly, glancing at me. "She didn't eat much."

This time my aunt's voice was quiet, too, and I could hear only the one side of the conversation.

"True," he murmured, nodding. "True."

I huddled on the steps, half listening. Below us, the cars were starting to line up at the curb. Small cars, station wagons, SUVs, minivans, a motorcycle, several sedans.

"If I catch the four-fifteen," said my uncle, "I can be at the hospital by eight. Tell her to wait till eight!"

He laughed. He wiped his eyes.

Above us, the clouds stretched and shifted, gathering in bunches. I trained my eyes on the extending row of cars at the curbside. More were lining up every minute, passing through the street break into the tree-lined residential neighborhood nearby. I didn't usually sit on this side of the school, the Ash Street side, instead getting picked up by Alberta's mother or my mother on the other end with the smaller brick building, where the younger grades got out, and I had never watched the formation of the pickup line for the bigger kids before. I had never let the pickup line command all my focus, with nothing else to distract me, and no car of my own to drive off in.

As a game, a game I had played with myself many times before, I let the thing in front of me lose a little touch with itself. I liked to play it if my mother was late, or if I was at a birthday party where I didn't know the kid very well: to loosen my understanding of the relationships between things and try to see what was happening in front of me as if I did not know what it was. What was this colorful circle held by a parent and topped with lit candles? What were these shiny wrapped boxes all in a pile? How easily I slipped into it, the sensation that I had materialized from elsewhere, without handbook or experienced context.

"Listen to the nurse," my uncle whispered into the phone, his face now fully turned to the side.

From what I could understand, every car—and I did let myself recognize them as cars—had at least one adult in it, but was also incomplete. They were clearly waiting for something. They waited patiently in their long row, without jostling; it did not seem to matter who or what was at the front of the line. A few turned off their motors, but no one got out. Their business was with the car, required staying with the car, and it seemed as though they would be driving again soon.

What were they waiting for? Across the street stood houses and those restaurants, but no one was getting out to go home, or pick up food. It had to be related to the larger building where we were sitting, the one attached to the lawn with the sign on the front that read **Lewis and Clark Elementary**. Behind its front offices, one could glimpse a yellow slide on a yard and a handball court, so it seemed a reasonable guess to think that the building housed children. That this was a building full of children. At some point, via some cue, the children would have to emerge, and then something new would happen, something having to do with the cars. This was my hypothesis, and as a loud clanging reverberated in the air, the building doors flung open, and the stillness of the walls and the grass broke and filled fast with people, specifically children, everywhere, active, busy, kids running through the silver gates, tearing down the lawn, shouting, laughing. Every kid ran down the lawn and within a short number of minutes found a particular car, opened the car door, and threw its body inside. It happened over and over—kids pouring down the hills, knowing just where to go even if stalling and playing, no kid going for long into the wrong car, no car expunging its chosen child. Kids entering and shutting doors, kids receiving cups or snacks or nothing from the adult hand in the front seat, kids pulling straps over their bodies, and then each car driving away from the curb once it received its cargo. The car fulfilled completion once the correct child entered it, and then the car could go. In the new spaces provided, more drove up, and the line shifted and shortened, restructured its first, lengthened again, accepted children, shortened again; a fresh wave surged through doorways to dash down the lawn from other released classrooms, and the cycle went around a few times over a series of many energetic minutes, cars driving in, cars driving out, the choreography entirely predictable, almost synchronized, until at last only one remained, a silver sedan, engine humming. The woman in the driver's seat fiddled with the radio. I could see this by the movement of her arm. Finally, the last kid, running, whom I couldn't help but recognize because his younger sibling was also in my class and had already settled in the back, burst forth from the gates of the field with a gaping backpack, down the hill, across the sidewalk, to be swallowed by the sedan, and after straps were attached and both children were pressed into their spots, the woman stopped messing with the radio and pulled away. Then there was no trace of any of them: neither children nor cars, and only the expanse of green lawn, and trees, and some birds on the upper walkway pecking at crumbs left behind from lunches, crumbs that could never reattach to any bread or sandwich.

The totality of it all was horrible. I was not at that time and age truly cognizant of what was in play for me on that day, but the terror I suddenly felt at the empty lawn was real, and as I looked at it the whole thing, the whole lawn, seemed to tilt, like all the trees and grasses were leaning and listing even though nothing in my neck or head had moved. "Remember to breathe out," my uncle was whispering to my aunt, "exhale," and the words came at me sideways and I thought I might fall right off the ground, then, the untilted straight flat ground. It was like witnessing an eradication of children, the empty schoolfront, the plain green grass, the car line empty, the stretch of gray curb, like they had never been there and would never return, and the mobility of humanness struck me right then as something gross and foul, even despicable, so endlessly rolling and loose we were, so portable and untethered to anything. I tried to return myself to this world I lived in, to reinstate framework, **my** school, **my** pickup line, **my** mother's car, parked in our parking space in our apartment building only a few blocks away, but nothing held form and the ground kept its tilt and I couldn't seem to settle myself back into myself. I might've started tearing at things right then, pulling at my hair or clothes, touching my nose to the railing over and over like a goose or a broken toy, to feel I was there, to confirm thereness, if I had not glimpsed, right at that moment, in the middle of the lawn, a white rectangular piece of something that had drifted out of one of those backpacks during the absorption of the children into the cars.

I locked my eyes right on it. From a distance, it

was just that small shape of white, but I used every bit of it I could to fill my gaze, to edge out everything else. I stood, and left my uncle talking to my aunt. Into the slight breeze, the ruffling leaves. The empty curb running alongside. The lawn, the lawn, the lawn, the lawn, the lawn, the lawn, then the paper. It was far at the other end, by a cluster of hedges, and as I got closer it became increasingly itself, bigger, brighter and more papery, man-made, perfectly shaped with its four right-angled corners, damp from an afternoon mist that had come and gone, eight and a half by eleven, and looking so incredibly and beautifully like every other piece of paper I had ever before encountered. How worshipful I felt of it right then, this relic, this reminder of the existence of people, this connection between the school and the gone cars, as too I felt such a rush of love for the empty red metallic cinnamon candy wrapper I saw scuttling by over the blades of grass buoyed by the afternoon breeze.

For a little while, I sat there in front of the paper, being with it. When I finally flipped it over, it appeared to be a classroom handout from a science unit. Boxes contained printed illustrations of various beetles, labeled in a sloppy hand by an unreadable name in the top righthand corner. Mandible, abdomen, legs; longhorn beetle, weevil, stag.

The breeze fluttered its edges. I did not know then of course that this paper would extend its role in my life, that there was more to happen with it and its beetle emergence, but I could still feel rising off the page a luster of importance, and when I picked it up, I did it carefully, as if it were animal skin parchment, folding it in half like a teacher might before handing a solemn child a note to bring to the principal. I took it slowly back to my own backpack, where it fit in the front zipper pocket next to some dried-out markers and loose pen caps. My uncle, still on the phone, smiled at me again. He was listening to something long. I was young, and did not really know what it meant that he was waiting to be a father, that this was one of the biggest days of his life, but as I sat down on the roots of the nearby maple, I do remember flashing on Vicky for a second, fetal Vicky, unnamed baby, and how she was not yet in the world, but soon would be, and how once Vicky was out she too would be loose, like all the kids, and all the cars, and all the mothers, and everyone.

By the time my babysitter came out to find us, apologizing, tugging a green suitcase on rollers, my uncle was napping on the side steps, his head resting on the railing, snoring a little, and I was holding tight to my backpack, still sitting on the maple roots.

"I'm ready," the babysitter said, and my uncle shook awake, and they both walked me to her car.

13

As we approached the parking lot, teachers were emerging from the school, heading to their own cars. Mrs. Washington from the front office clicked by, wearing some kind of flamingo purse on her shoulder; the principal with the black-framed plastic glasses looked to the ground and spoke intently by a wall to the gym coach. These were the celebrities of my life. Mrs. Washington waved as she drove off: "Have a good weekend!" My uncle stood next to me with a hand on my shoulder as the babysitter settled her bag into the trunk. "I'll see you in a few days," he said, "Francie," and the babysitter opened the passenger door for me, and the car, smelling of grapes, with fake leopard-skin seat covers, and a pink-haired troll hanging by a string from the rearview mirror, absorbed me inside.

14

The steward/cousin my uncle secured for me for the train ride would turn out to be, as promised, extremely nice, and dependable, and also tall and lanky with a giant Adam's apple so knobby it had made me laugh. At night on the train, he reminded me that he had the sleeper next door and all I had to do was knock if I needed anything, anything at all. "I sleep lightly," he said. "If you have nightmares and need company or whatever. We can go to the hall or back to the seats. Please don't worry about waking me." He didn't smile, but his neutral face was warm. Still, even with kindness so palpable, on the train, in the hallways, I never knocked on the steward's door in the middle of the night to have him read me passages from his whaling book largely because I did not need to. I had been right about the train, and its pace. I loved my sleeper car, and any disturbances I felt or had to cry out were things I wanted to manage, anyway, on my own. By that point, I'd eaten the butterfly, and was soon to hold the beetle in my palms, and visitors were coming on and off the train, asking for things, and the whole trip was like a dream fog, me moving down the line drawn in the dirt by Uncle Stan's stick, from pebble to pebble, a line which itself had surely washed away with the rain I'd heard tapping on the roof of the babysitter's apartment as I lay tucked under the slippery chenille blanket on her couch, golden butterflies circling on the lampshade beside me.

Soon after the train ride was completed, I was settling into my new home in Burbank, California, sitting in the kitchen nook, eating a bowl of cereal, when the steward's father, Tony, Uncle Stan's cousin, a man I'd never met, made some joke on the phone about my mother and the loony bin. Uncle Stan had been using speakerphone, chatting about his life, holding the baby as he talked, and so we all heard everything, and he looked at me chewing up my cereal bits, and at his wife, sitting across from me with her alert eyes, wrapped in her wool cardigan, and quietly hung up. "I'm so sorry," he said, shaking his head. From what I understood, he sent news through the family mill that he would like an apology and waited for Tony to call back, but Tony did not believe in apologies and thought my uncle was being too sensitive. Time passed, grudges thickened, and the two of them, steward and Tony, became a ghost branch on the family tree. This was a source of sadness for my uncle, but it made some kind of basic sense to me. The steward shepherded me to Los Angeles, and then dissolved. In my child's mind, that was the whole of his existence anyway.

15

Do you like the radio?

It's okay.

I know this must be so confusing, Francie.

Is this your car?

Yes.

It's green.

It is. I like green.

Do you always drive this car?

I do. Do you like it?

I do.

I'm glad. That's my lucky troll. We'll have a couple good days of just you and me before the train ride. It's Friday! Weekend ahead. I know a great pancake place for tomorrow morning. Do you like pancakes?

Yes.

We'll get in line early. They have the most amazing syrup. It's a kind of special berry, you know those marionberries? Marionberry. They're those really long blackberries, so long and skinny, like someone pulled a blackberry and stretched it. Delicious. And we will talk to your aunt and uncle every day, okay?

My mom?

She can't talk to you just yet. As soon as she is better and she can talk, you will definitely talk to her. That's the glove compartment.

Can I open it?

It's messy in there. You don't usually sit in the front, do you?

What's this?

Just Advil. Yeah, that should stay there. I probably should've put you in the back but it's so messy, too. Would you rather sit in the back?

No.

Sorry, that's just an old fork. I don't know why that's there.

Shrina?

Yes?

When do I go?

Sunday. Sunday morning.

And will I talk to my mom then?

Not yet, Francie. God. I'm really sorry. They said not yet. Probably not by Sunday. It's going to take her a little while to feel better enough to talk.

What's this for?

Those are the papers I need for the car. Insurance and stuff. Careful. I do need those.

Is this gum?

Yeah, I think it's kind of old.

Can I have a piece?

I think it's too old. I mean, oh, okay. If you really want. Sure.

Where do they live?

Your aunt and uncle? In Los Angeles. Didn't they tell you you were going to live with them? For now at least? Just push it back up to close it. Push and close. Thanks. Let me just park. This is me, right here. You see the little window on top? Have you ever been to a loft?

No.

Then I will get to show you one. I'm so glad.

They told me. He told me.

He seems really nice.

The gum tastes weird.

Just spit in my hand, Francie. There you go. Come up the stairs. Let's get you settled.

This is the living room, Francie. This is the kitchen. It's really small. Up there is the loft. I sleep up there. Can you see the bed?

Yes.

It's called a loft, that whole upstairs area on top of the ladder. Are you hungry?

No.

I might have some cookies. Do you like cookies?

Is this your lamp?

The butterfly lamp? It is. Do you like it?

Yes.

Have a seat. On the couch, or chair. Wherever. Make yourself at home. Have you ever heard that expression?

No.

It means, feel comfortable here. Like—make it like it's your own home. Where is that bag of cookies. I mean, what do you do at home most days, when you come home from school?

Play cards maybe.

Cards. I don't think I have cards.

Watch a show.

I have a TV, over on that table, under the fringy scarf—do you think there's a show you like on now?

I don't know.

Do you know how to look for it?

No.

Okay, hang on. I'm going to get the cookies first. Food first. I was always so hungry when I came home from school. I swear I would eat a whole loaf of toasted bread with butter. Cookies, cookies, cookies. Where are you, cookies! Crackers, no. Do you like crackers? Oh, here! And, plate.

Plate, plate, plate.

Exactly! And, wait. Let me get you a napkin.

I like the lamp.

I'm so glad. My mother got it for me when I was a little girl. Here, let me turn it on.

The butterflies are so red.

Aren't they?

And golden.

And, here you are. Why don't you come on over. Milk? I have some soy milk.

Okay.

Go ahead and sit—the couch is good. This couch is very soft. I pick my couches for softness. There you go. I swear I sat on every couch in the store! They were ready to throw me out. Help yourself. Have as many as you'd like.

It's good.

I'm so glad, Francie. Have you had soy milk before?

I don't know.

It's vanilla flavored. Do you like vanilla?

Yes.

Okay, let me just listen to my messages for a minute. You good?

Yes. Thank you.

Of course, sweetie.

Where did your mother get the lamp from?

Just listening for a second. Hang on. My brother called. He's in New York.

The soy milk is good.

Good, good. And, erase. And then—my bank. E-rase. And, then Susie. My friend.

Is that Susie from school?

Different Susie. Hang on. And, erase.

Did she make the lamp?

The Butterfly Lampshade

My mother? I believe she bought it at a department store. Did your uncle say he'll stay at the hospital with the baby tonight?

What is the name of the store?

I don't know, probably Robinson's. She used to really like Robinson's. Why?

Is there a Robinson's near here?

You want to see where my mother bought the lamp?

Yes.

Why, Francie?

I like it.

That's so nice of you. I'll tell my mother. She'll be very pleased. What do you like about it?

The butterflies on it.

You want one of your own.

Yes.

This was years and years ago. I mean, I don't know if they have them anymore. I don't even think Robinson's exists anymore. Does it? But—you'll be sleeping on this couch. You can sleep right next to it.

Here?

I can leave it on at night if you'd like. Do you like a light at night?

Okay.

Great. You can watch the butterflies if you wake up. It's a soft bulb. It'll be perfect. Did you have enough cookies?

Yes, thank you.

Great. Let's find your show. I need to do a little work but you can watch and I can work and then we'll hang out. How does that sound?

Good.

And we'll talk to your aunt and uncle later with an update on your mom. And the baby!

Shrina, when I go, can I take the lamp?

You'll have a brand-new cousin! Wow. You will be such an amazing help to them.

Can I take it with me?

Sorry, take what with you?

The lamp.

Take the lamp? You mean with you on the train?

I could put it in a box.

Oh, gosh, I'm so sorry, Francie. It's just—it's a gift from my childhood. I feel like I should keep it.

That's okay.

I'm sorry. I should probably just give it to you—

Okay.

But it's like the only thing from a certain time, from when my parents divorced. Just it's special to me. I'm so glad you like it. You can visit it anytime.

Me?

Of course, you. It could be your special lamp to visit.

But how?

I mean, whenever you are in town, you can come visit it. Is this the show?

No. Will I be in town?

Oh, I'm sure you will. Your aunt and uncle will bring you up here to see your mother.

Isn't it far?

I mean, yeah, it's a little far, but they will come up here. Of course they will. This one? The squirrels?

I don't like that one. When will I visit?

I don't know, Francie.

Every week?

No, probably not every week. Maybe every month? Every other month?

And then I can visit the lamp.

The lamp, anytime. You can come see it every visit, absolutely.

Even on a weekend?

Definitely. Definitely on a weekend.

That one's okay.

This one? The lions?

Yes.

Here you go. Okay. It's ready. You ready? Do you want to talk more?

No. Why are you crying?

I'm not crying. I don't know, am I? Just a little. I just—I just want you to have a good trip. You're a good kid.

I'm not.

You are, Francie. You are very good.

I just imagined something bad.

You did? What did you imagine?

I can't tell you.

Of course you can. You can tell me anything.

You were burning in a fire.

Oh, sweetie. Really? Oh, wow. You've had a tough day.

And you were yelling a little I think. And burning.

It's okay. It's okay. Where did you see something like that?

And I was laughing or something.

Did you watch a show for grown-ups?

I just saw it in my mind.

Okay. Okay. Well, you didn't burn me, see? I'm fine. I'm regular temperature. I'm not hurt at all.

Are you sure?

I'm sure, I'm sure. Look, I'm fine. Okay? Would you like me to watch with you a little bit?

I maybe also threw a knife at you.

I will watch with you a little bit, okay?

This one is good. This is where they go to school.

I would really like to watch it with you.

The teacher is funny. She's a rabbit.

We'll just sit here together and watch it.

Okay.

Okay.

Sorry I said that. I don't really want you to burn up.

I understand, Francie. It's okay. I don't plan on burning up. Let's watch the show.

16

"I have had many female inspirations in my life so far, including my theater teacher, my mother, and an amazing nurse who helped me in the hospital when I tore my shoulder ligament. But my biggest inspiration is, without question, my sister. She moved to our house when she was eight years old because her mother suffers from mental illness plus an early head injury. I was only a baby at the time, so I always remember her with us, but sometimes she will tell me stories about her other life, when she was a little girl living in Portland, and what it was like with her mother then. She said mostly it was nice, but when her mother wasn't well, she'd start knitting blankets all the time, or ask Francie what her name was. Or once, her mother (my aunt) handed her a half-opened jar of pickles to give as a present at a birthday party. My sister hid it under the stairs and went to the party without anything.

"My mother always took me shopping before friends' birthday parties. We went to toy stores together, and as we browsed the aisles, she asked me what I'd like to get for my friend, and sometimes I'd even get something too.

"My sister laughs when I tell her she's my hero. She even snorts a little, like it's not true.

"She's fun, and easy to be with, and I've never seen her do anything truly worrisome, but soon after she arrived at our house, when I was a very little baby, she asked our mom to put a lock on her door. Not a regular lock from the inside, for privacy, but on the outside. To lock her in. When our mom asked why, she said she just wanted to feel safe in there. She said that sometimes she sleepwalked and she didn't want to leave the room in the middle of the night and fall down the stairs, though no one had ever seen anything close to that happen. Our mom didn't like it, but she ended up buying the lock because Francie doesn't ask for much. For years, Mom was the one who opened her door up in the morning, but when I was old enough and had to get up earliest for school, it became my job to unlock Francie from her bedroom. Every morning my alarm would ring, I'd get out of bed, and the first thing I'd do would be to walk over to her door and turn the little locking device so that she could come out.

"I can't say I understand why she wanted that. But it was an honor to release her. To be the one to unlock the door in the morning, and return her to our family and daily life. My mother always thought it was upsetting, and worried, but Francie seemed happy about it, and I have always liked that I was given such an important task.

"I also think of college like a door you have to unlock. Inside are so many mysteries about the world, and I am excited to take on that job, the job of opening up one of those doors and seeing what's inside. We are all locked in rooms in different ways, and part of growing up is finding different kinds of keys, and meeting the people who will help free you. I feel my experience with my sister has opened me up already to many of the ways I am lucky in the world. I want to learn all I can, and open all I can, and make my parents, and my sister, proud."

17

After the Sunday dinner at Aunt Minn's, over the course of the rest of that week, I tried to double my stock for the online object shop and increase speed of delivery. I wanted to create a new photography corner in my apartment, and after work took the bus to the fabric store to buy a yard apiece of a few colors of velvet—deep red, royal blue, midnight black, and silvery white, because most objects look their finest when placed upon velvet. I tried a few corners until I'd settled on one across from the balcony where the early morning sunlight was indirect and golden, fresh and also forgiving, and after careful placement, retook photographs of some of the objects I hadn't yet sold, reposting them with new names and pictures, and within a few hours had found buyers for three, including an old-fashioned adorable bear to a young woman in Nevada, and a small metal mare I'd found just a few days earlier, so noble on its pasture of red velvet, to an older gentleman in Visalia, who said it reminded him of a beloved toy from his childhood. I sketched a business logo of a vase on a rock, and sent it away to some company that would make stickers which I would then use to seal the tissue paper I wrapped around each item, plus another matching sticker of my PO box information for the return addresses. I went to the art store and invested in an improved selection of tissue paper, all colors, and some more bubble wrap, and ordered four bricks of mushroom Styrofoam to give it a try. I changed my site backdrop to a lively plaid.

To continue to keep the days simple, I did not invite anyone over, or follow up on any plans, though I did tell Vicky again that she was always welcome.

I had officially quit the framing job the day after I had given the customer her completed beetle in its gilded frame. "It's magnificent," she'd said as I unwrapped it and we looked at it together. Right in the middle of the frame, perfectly centered. Inert. Something about seeing it under glass had made me feel ill, and when the woman walked out the door, the package rewrapped and tucked under her arm, ready to check it off her to-do list and out of her mind perhaps forever, I went to get my backpack and held it at my desk and when the clock changed to five, on my way out, I told my boss that this had been my last day and that I was truly regretful to give her such little notice but that framing was just not for me. "I'm very sorry," I said again. "I cannot return." My boss stared at me in confusion, but before she could respond, I left the building, and although I did not like to think of myself as the type of person who would leave her workplace and her coworkers in the lurch, the moment I walked into the glaring rays of afternoon on Victory, the cars driving by, the traffic lights tall and steady, the sun a blast of concentrated heat in contrast with the all-day monolithic chill of air-conditioning, I felt like shouting. On the walk home, I found a free curbside wooden CD shelf that might work well for somebody's knickknacks, and hauled it under my arm, turning the corner onto Chandler, lifting it up the stairs, wiping it down as soon as I stepped in the door. There was a new and focused energy in me, that was for sure. With every step I took away from those right-angled corners and meaning-making shapes, it did seem that something was continuing to loosen.

It all left space, is what it did. Lots of space, and unfilled hours. Once my new rhythm settled in, I would likely be busier than before, but I would be bound only to the schedules supplied by the yard sales, and the open/closed limitations of the post office, and about other things that took up time, I could be more particular. I would, for example, I told myself, tidying up the corners of the new piles of cheerful tissue paper, making little stacks so that I could easily access different colors, hold off on anything resembling a relationship, or a date. It had been good to hear that my mother was courting someone; I, however, would not. At the nearby Ralphs, close to my apartment, I often stood in line to have my food run through the sensors by an affable checker with oak bark–colored eyes and capable hands who liked to tell me when I asked about the cloud patterns—nimbus, cumulus, none. Sometimes, he floated questions with interest in his face that another person or even a future self might enjoy answering. I moved away from the tissue paper and laid out all the different kinds of tape: clear, packing, iridescent for special sales. I liked that man at Ralphs, I thought to myself, settling the tapes in their spots, placing a stapler at the edge, but there was no place for him at this current stage, and as the sunlight reached through the balcony window and brightened the side walls, illuminating the wall cracks like little lightning bolts, storming the light switch, this did not strike me as bleak, or lonely, but right, and real, and like the recent texting with that friend about the made-up trip to Portland that had shut down any further questions from her and given me the space to do as I pleased, I could titrate the interactions with the checker at Ralphs in such a way as to leave nothing loose. What for another person might feel lonely and damaging would be, right now, for me, a kind of vitamin. I arranged the Styrofoam peanut packing supplies in another corner, next to the assortment of folded boxes. One must, at certain times in a life, burrow, I thought, standing up. The new packing and shipping area was ready to go. Clouds belong to open air.

I photographed the CD shelf with a few well-chosen knickknacks (also for sale) to demonstrate its efficacy, selling it within two days to a buyer in Butte who collected small milkmaid sculptures that needed a display case, and while I worked on perfecting my email manners to reply to customers, and fine-tuning my packing to fit more sales within each day, I also looped, on and off, around Vicky's sticky memory idea. The conversation from Sunday's dinner had been living right with me. How could I make that work? Why was what she had said so interesting to me? The idea for a structure started to emerge on its own, and by Friday, I called Vicky up and asked her if she was willing to take me on Saturday to shop at a lumberyard for a few beams, and to the nearby fabric store for canvas and sturdy zippers. It was scheduled to be a hot weekend, into the triple digits. "I can't carry it all," I told her, "and it's related to something you said." By that point, the image of the tent was fairly clear to me. Four sides, triangle top, one-person-sized. "About Mom?" "About the sticky memories," I said. "About cheese?" "It's a new project," I said. "It'll be easier to explain in person. Oh, can you bring your toolkit? We'll need to build a little. And you know that old rose? Would it be possible to bring that too?" "What rose?" "You know the old one from long ago that I put in the trash?" "You mean the magic rose?" "I just thought we could dust the canvas with it or something. I don't know. Just have it be there for a moment." "Okay." "You still have it?" "Francie." "Oh, and bring a copy of the essay, too, if you'd like. We can work on that after."

Early on Saturday morning, before Vicky came by, I went to a couple more sales in the neighborhood, easy walks away, in which I found an expensive crystal pitcher that the seller wanted to get rid of for cheap as it was reflecting prismatically all the pain of her divorce, a quality ukulele, two broken but fixable iPods, and an assortment of outrageous costume jewelry made of celluloid blue triangles that if photographed correctly (on silver-white velvet) could be priced very well. Due to the heat, the sales had started early to catch the motivated buyers—I had my choices in hand by eight a.m., walking home before the vicious sun started marching up the sky.

Vicky picked me up after lunch in Aunt Minn's sedan, and we drove together to the lumberyard. She'd stopped at a convenience store on the way to buy a large-size bag of shelled sunflower seeds, her favorite, as if we were on a road trip, and she tossed them in her mouth as we talked, giving updates from the week, including how Aunt Minn had agreed to let her go to the pool party the next day as long as she promised to come home right after and not to drink anything, **anything,** from any punch bowl, to which Vicky had said she had never in her life been to a party with a punch bowl, and who could fit such a thing into a cabinet anyway. “They’re huge, right?” she asked. “Huge,” I said, not knowing. We pulled into the parking lot of the lumberyard. The storefront loomed ahead with its brown and assertive lettering. “The rose is in here,” she said, patting her backpack on the center console. “I wrapped it in tissue. It’s really delicate.” “Thank you,” I said, “truly.” As Vicky tugged up the parking brake, I told her I wanted to try to explain to her what we were doing, why we were here, how more of these memories had been leaking into my thinking, almost formlessly, so we sat in our bucket seats and I described some of what I’d been recalling over the week about my mother and the hammer smashing, and the details of that day of change in general. How I wanted to spend more time with those memories. How her “sticky” idea had stayed with me. Vicky ate one sunflower seed at a time, listening with her attentive gold eyes, chewing, and outside the windshield, the store was a fixed presence, a goal that was allowing me to tell her, because every word I said was pressured, helpfully, by the knowledge that we would soon be leaving the car. Vicky shook her head, and said she hadn’t even really known it was a hammer smashing, of my mother’s hand? really? and I told her how her father had flown in on the day of her birth and picked me up in the main office and had taken me to lunch before rushing back to fly home to meet her. "You mean me?" "You." "You're saying it was my birthday?" "Exactly. He had a chicken burrito," I added. "And a coffee." I put my fingers on the door handle, and then so did she, like I'd given us both permission to leave, and we exited together into the scathing heat of midday, with Vicky keeping the sunflower seed bag with her, because it seemed to be offering some sort of modulating role in her experience, whatever that was. She reached out to hug me on a cement island in the parking lot, and her face was sad, saying it was hard to imagine this about me as a little kid, when she was just a baby, and how scary it all must've been, but as we approached the building, and I continued to fill in the story, she jumped to open the electric doors and let out a kind of amazed bark. "But, I mean," she said, "the level of detail is outrageous. Sugar packets? Alberta's paper dolls? I know you have a good memory, but you can't possibly recall all of this." Inside, the store was beautifully air-conditioned, and we strolled the aisles, passing rows of golden pine boards and planks, looking for smaller beams they could saw to size to establish what would become the four ends of the tent. She offered me the bag and I ate a few of the seeds too, though I've never really liked them, their insipid grayness, and I lied and told Vicky no, of course I didn't remember all of it, that I was just making up some stuff on the spot to make it more interesting for her.

"I like the details," she said. "Don't get me wrong. It's just that it's impossible for anyone to remember that closely."

We carried the beams to the outside back area, where the carpenter sawed them to my specifications, and down the street, at the fabric store, I found a roll of orange canvas, and some long sturdy zippers wrapped in plastic casing. I wanted the tent to be orange, and canvas, with four ends, and a triangular shape. I had briefly explained the structure to Vicky as we did the shopping, asking also for her building expertise, since she'd made a few sets in her play production courses. "Does it have to be exactly like this?" she asked at the cashier's counter, licking salt off her fingers, and I told her yes, yes, it did. That I wasn't sure why, but it did. We carried the bags to her car. As she drove, she kept circling her free arm because she'd injured her shoulder removing the lighting gels from the last show, and for a while, we sat in silence, her arm moving through space like a lever, until it pulled something up and she started telling me about her own earliest memory, how it had been someone's skirt, likely her mom's, such a crimson swirling red, and how part of the hem had been coming loose and she could recall picking at the tiny red threads. "I guess at a party?" Then we parked and unpacked, and she showed me a photo on her phone of the guy she was currently liking in history class, the one who would hopefully be at the pool party, and the girl who was likely to land the role of Emily. I lugged the bags upstairs to spare her shoulder. At the top of the staircase, I could see the cars tooling on the streets below us, going about their days. The canvas smelled good. The orange shade was just right. Vicky was walking slowly up the stairs to meet me, absorbed in writing a text on her phone, her toolkit tucked under her arm, and I felt, as I had so many times before, a wave of almost overwhelming relief and appreciation at her existence.

On the balcony, we pulled the canvas off its roll to stretch it for size against the back wall. I made a rough sketch on drafting paper and showed Vicky how I wanted the wood to stand; we had the rest of the afternoon to put it together, with a pizza arriving midway. Vicky got absorbed with setting up songs to play for us on her phone, and then, to the spring of pop music, she set the four planks into their spots and stood back to plan her approach. It was dry and hot, but the balcony was mostly shaded by a large ficus that had been breaking up the sidewalk with its roots for years, and I set up a standing fan in the living room that rotated and blew air to us through the opening in the glass door. While we worked, we went back and forth to the freezer in the kitchen to refill our waters with ice.

In my corner, I cut the canvas at its marked lines, and brought out a sewing kit to use to attach the zipper. The two of us worked companionably, mostly silent, sometimes singing along. Vicky is the person with whom I have done the most side-by-side activities in my life; we often studied together on the living room couch, or more often in her bedroom, me against one wall, her at her desk, then on her bed, then next to me, with her elaborate and sometimes glue-heavy elementary school projects, me plowing through various high school essays and test preparations. On the balcony, she hummed and surveyed the shape, trying out a few approaches for the top, finally deciding on a kind of gathered middle with the "door" in front, facing the balcony railing. She placed the planks and began to drill some holes. I finished the zipper attachment; the stitches were uneven and jerky, like stitches in a cartoon, but the zipper held, and I ran it up and down a few times, satisfied. After she'd set the screws, we took a break for pizza, and more ice water, and then washed our hands free of grease, and she waved off any offers to take a break to look at her essay, absorbed, she said, in this today, just this.

As the final step, we draped the canvas into place, and nailed it in at key corners and sides. At my request, she brought out the old rose from her backpack, unwrapping the tissue around it like inside was a series of tiny bones. It looked so crinkly and old and brownish, the petals almost cracking, and with careful hands, we moved it up and down the panels like someone waving sage through the rooms of a new house. Not cleansing, though. Orienting, maybe. "Like that?" she said, moving it inside and outside the tent, and I laughed a little and said sure. It was all a little humiliating. I found I could hardly even stand to look at the rose, which I had found in my adolescence at the base of the curtains at Deena's house, and which Vicky herself had rescued from the garbage bin a few days after that. When she finished waving it around, she folded it back into its tissue and returned it to her backpack. The sun had set, and in the bluing light of evening, the serene coolness of the valley spreading out like a balm, Vicky leaned against me, and we stood back to survey our work.

It was a sturdy boxy structure, a one-person-sized space big enough for the triangular shape of myself sitting. "Cool," said Vicky, bobbing her head. It all looked a little like a joke. She'd done good work with the nailing, and the pulling together of the canvas up top, but it still looked like something made in a few hours by people who didn't really know what they were doing; this was especially true for me, but although she had done a functional job, Vicky had never built an actual structure before in set-building class—that had been more about large wooden panels for backdrops, and never anything so small. It was, by all accounts, a first attempt for us both. Vicky asked if I was going to try it out, or if she could, and I told her that I would wait until the morning but it was okay if she did just this one time, and she bent down solemnly and crawled in.

Zipped it up. I stood on the balcony and gathered up the debris of our efforts: the leftover shreds of canvas, the sawdust from the planks, all the time aware of her there and not there, her enclosed presence so close to me and also, like a formalized version of the body, far away, separate. I fetched a broom to sweep up the area, thinking about how much I liked the idea of giving the memories a place to emerge, like they had an inherent gaseous nature, and the tent would prevent them from floating away. I had not dared say this aloud to her, but it was without question part of my own thinking. Vicky stayed inside for a few minutes, longer than I'd expected, and when the zipper moved down on its own, and she emerged like a little bright-eyed pink-cheeked birthed calf, she said as she hauled herself out that it actually did seem a little different somehow than just sitting and remembering in a regular chair or whatever other people did when they wanted to think about stuff, and she thought she could maybe feel things coming to her just by sitting in it—"murky things, like this mysterious mist," and that she was now, despite her previous confusions, a little excited for me. "When will you start?" "Tomorrow," I said. "You'll tell me how it goes?" "I will." "You won't stay in there forever?" "I won't. Not at all." "You'll check in with us regularly?" "I promise."

"It's going to be hot in there," she said, wiping her forehead. "You might need some kind of hand fan."

That night, in bed, staring at the ceiling, in my room, door locked, tent on the balcony adding its weight to the apartment, a subtle weight I thought I could feel, I made myself a plan. While I was using this tent, it seemed valuable to continue to keep my regimen as simple as possible. I had abandoned the framing job, so as long as I could maintain paying my bills, the way I organized my time would stay my own. I would try to wake up and go to the tent in the earliest hours of morning, even before sunrise if possible, in the very coolest part of the day, and once inside I would sit and surely daydream and think about other things and make lists for the mailings but still try, as much as I could, to let the memories take shape, to attempt, bit by bit, to make what had been a blur more defined, described and shaped by care and attention. I wanted to focus mostly on the period of time that had started with the hammer smashing and ended with my arrival in Burbank, California, including the visit from my uncle, the stay with the babysitter, and the train ride with the steward, and also of course the parallel entrances of the butterfly in the water glass, the beetle on the paper, and many years later, those roses under the curtain. This would be my project, though I did realize other memories might arise, and that memories were not soldiers, lined up in tidy rows. That would be okay. I would see how it went. I would not wear a timer or wear a watch once inside so that the chamber itself would be separate from time, like a casino but with nothing in it. Like a tiny triangular empty moneyless canvas silent casino. As the car lights from down the street swirled against the wall of my bedroom, making patterns and lighting up blinds, I thought how it would be a kind of second job—not a paying job, but not unlike standing in the playground and taking stock of my internal state, though an internal state of the past, a reinsertion of myself into past events, especially because at the time of the events, I had barely been aware of what was going on. I wanted to track it. That's all I wanted to do. The bedroom was quiet, and comforting. If I strained my ears, I thought I could hear the soft tones of my next-door neighbor Jose and his wife talking next door. One of their rooms shared a wall with mine. I could never make out the words, but I could hear their presences, her higher tones and giddy laugh, his low and formal murmurings. He would come unlock my bedroom door in the morning before he went to work at the racetrack, where he was head horse wrangler, usually around four in the morning. It was almost the first of the month, which meant I owed him cash, so I made a note to stop at the bank the next day to take out the money needed. Fifty dollars a month. On the list of my expenses, a line item in my budget. To break the twenty, I would buy myself some of that quality beef jerky at the convenience store near the ATM, and something about imagining putting the two twenties and the ten into an envelope, and folding the envelope to feed it into the slot that was Jose's mailbox downstairs, and placing the beef jerky on my kitchen counter, and in this way renewing the month, was adequately soothing to send me to sleep.

18

"Who's that?" Vicky asks once, when I wave to Jose one Saturday afternoon after he calls out a hi, mounting the outside staircase of the building with bags of groceries in his arms. She and I are heading out to get ice cream at the Rite Aid/former Thrifty's down the street, the last place for miles to find real rainbow sherbet.

"Just a neighbor friend," I tell her. She gives me one of her hopeful looks. "As in, friend. He's married. Happily married. He helps me out with stuff. That's all." "He seems nice." "He's very nice. Very helpful."

19

On the Monday after the tent's construction, I woke up earlier than usual, five a.m. probably, with a kind of giddy anticipation, like one might feel on the morning of a new school year, or a new and exciting job. Jose had already unlocked my bedroom door and driven off in his truck to Santa Anita. I stood formally and opened the door into the rest of the apartment. The living room was dark, the boxes and piles of supplies darker forms on the floor, and I picked my way through them to the glass door of the balcony. Outside, the streets below were empty. Streetlamps still lit. Storefronts closed. I flipped up the balcony door's lock and quietly slid the glass open.

Against the back wall of the balcony, in the darkness, the tent rested in its spot like a child's fort. Lumpy, and awkward, and odd. There was no real reason to do this, I thought, standing, staring at it. It was a silly construction. This was not something people did with their time. I stepped onto the balcony, and glancing around, as if someone might be watching, squatted and unzipped its entry panel, crawled in, and zipped it back up. My heart, to my surprise, was beating hard. I imagined someone catching me, saying I was violating building codes, or that it wasn't allowed, this kind of action; it wasn't right; it was, in some basic way, unseemly. Inside, it smelled strongly of new canvas, and the freshly cut sawed ends of the wood, and what I imagined was the faintest hint of aged paranormal rose, and I rotated around so that I was facing the balcony railing, even though all I could see were the darkened panels of what was the orange canvas, my poorly attached zipper, and the edges of Vicky's well-nailed beams. Downstairs, someone turned on their car and began backing out of a parking space. Something about it all was terribly, almost embarrassingly, private. I wasn't sure what to do. I could hear my own breathing, in and out, the body and its tasks, and I sat there quietly for a few minutes, and then closed my eyes. I may have dozed off a little. Around me, in the state between sleeping and waking, the intensity of light started to change, and as the sun began to rise and extend rays over the valley, the orange of the tent picked up a faint glow that steadily grew brighter, and warmer. The walls flushed around me, fleshy and active, and more cars began their routes through the streets, the sounds of traffic blending into an ambient soundtrack of the city waking up, more neighbors backing out of their designated slots in the parking lot, honking, accelerating. It was Monday morning. The memories were so close. They were ready to go. Sitting on the steps, staying with the babysitter, packing up my things, getting to the train. A faint wave of panic passed through me, like I might burst and explode shreds through the canvas, but my body didn't move, and I didn't leave, and more than anything, as I sat there, it seemed like I had gone to all these lengths to do what was really the most obvious thing in the world for me to do, because for all my talk of forgetting with Vicky, of tacitly agreeing falsely that I was adding details to embellish the story for her enjoyment, of not answering her when she said it was all impossible, my memory of this time is keen. It is keen. That is not bragging; that is merely descriptive. Once I pay attention, it is all right there to consider, and I have made up nothing. That's the whole point.

That morning, I spent a little time in the tent, just beginning to think about when my uncle came to visit, and sitting on the steps with him at the elementary school, noticing how the memories rose up, and then submerged, and then rose up, and then submerged, and when I started to feel tired, I exited. Zipped it back up. There seemed to be something important about zipping it back up. I returned to the inside of my apartment and closed the glass balcony door, and before I began the rest of my day, to throw myself into the extremely above-the-surface actions of packaging objects and taking them to the post office, I looked out at it. Orange, and lumpy, and still. Absurd as it was, I already felt it looked a little different. Then I went to the living room and attended to boxes for several hours before heading to the post office to mail everything away.

PART TWO

Locks

20

My mother was the best and the worst at Go Fish. She was the best because she made the room into an ocean, our cushions a fishing boat—cutting lines of string to hang from the sides as we held our cards high to catch the dim glow of the corner lamp. While we were playing, she would sneakily attach something to one of my strings. "Do you have any fours?" I'd ask. "Sorry, darling. Go fish," she'd say, and after picking my card, I'd pull at the string to discover some kind of a small toy, a treasure from the depths of the beige carpet-sea, a tiny plastic frog, a crayon. The delight! I won every game we played of Go Fish, and not because she was letting me win, and not because she was a clueless player, but because she simply did not want to take my cards. She liked to give me all her cards. She hoarded her nines and she surely knew I had a nine but she never asked for my nine until I demanded hers and she gave me all three, and then the look on her face, the plainness of the pleasure.

Aunt Minn would tell me about this sometimes, about how everyone worried about her sister but that when she could, in the phases of health, my mother tucked Minn into her bed, and sang her made-up melodies, and gathered little treasures she'd found, flowers, pretty rocks, discarded toys at the playground, loose and sparkling beads. This same Go Fish game with treats tied to strings had originated with Minn, in their home in Corvallis, on their living room carpet, which had been, more suitably, blue. She'd been a lousy player then, too. "I always won," said Minn, tapping at the edge of her glass of wine. There we were again, in the living room, Vicky asleep upstairs, Uncle Stan working at the computer upstairs, my aunt and I at sea on the sofas. Was it coincidence that she too liked to sit at night in a dark living room near the glow of a distant lamp? It was like a small homage we made together, and I sometimes felt a flash of clarity then of how Minn and I shared something highly specific, how perhaps I had been a renewal of her to my mother, or how she had been a practice round for the arrival of me. "You can go to bed if you want to, Francie," my aunt said, gazing out the living room window, which had turned flat with interior light and impenetrable. "Can I stay?" "Of course. It's not boring to you, just sitting here?" "No. No."

21

After my TV show ended, the babysitter gave me a quick tour of her loft. At the high end of a wooden ladder, she showed me her mattress, messy with colorful blankets and pillows, shrouding an alarm clock and a few books tucked tight into a corner. The loft hung partway over the living room, which she'd furnished with a sofa, a TV draped in a scarf, a standing plant, and a spring green table that made the transition into kitchenette. "Here is the fridge," she said, back on the floor, pretending to be a person on a game show, flourishing, "please help yourself. You can eat anything in here." On her refrigerator were photographs of a few smiling people, whom I couldn't have cared less about, but they were held in place by magnets of cat faces: gray, black, tabby, rough to the touch. On the table next to the sofa she'd turned on that golden softly lit lamp with the butterflies, which I already felt belonged to me in some way, was mine on a much deeper level than just who happened to pay money at some store, and the lamp shared space with a clear jar filled with multicolored glass candies that later, when she wasn't looking, I carried around in my mouth. "Would you like any lemonade?" the babysitter asked, but I told her no.

There was no time for sipping. I was far too busy carefully touching my finger to the bowl of small woolen bananas she had set next to the matching bowl of big real bananas in the center of the spring green table. "That's for the tiny people," she whispered to me, winking. But what wasn't? A whiskered ceramic panda sat on the bathroom sink sprouting, from inside its head, several toothbrushes, including a wrapped one from her dentist that she said I was welcome to use. On a ledge, she had picked a few lush hydrangeas from the front walkway and gathered them bluely together in a vase made from an old juice jar cleared of its label.

"It's not much," she said, bowing a little, "but I hope it'll be a good place for you in transit."

Her voice was lit up by its usual warmth and energy, and she either did not remember or chose not to be worried about the violent daydreams I'd mentioned aloud, which neither of us brought up again.

I stood in the middle of the apartment, holding the glass of lemonade she had poured for me anyway. Her drinking glass was clear but had some kind of false bottom so it looked like the lemonade had been poured onto a bed of blue glass stones. "Is that your **ice**?" I'd asked, incredulous, and she'd laughed, gently. "This must all seem so strange to you," she said, "your babysitter's apartment," but I stood as still as I could with my glass in both hands and my bag by the sofa, and for a moment, imagined at the end of the weekend all the trains chugging past us until the station was empty and we walked back to her loft together where I would stay for a time while my mother got better, becoming, to the babysitter, not her child, no, but some sort of young roommate she would entirely take care of.

It occurs to me now that they surely paid her, but that was not something that entered my mind at the time.

I sat at the green table and did my homework while she made us dinner, grilled cheese and tomato soup. After we cleaned up and took a tour of her shoes—strappy purple sandals, worn-heeled black cowboy boots—I brushed my teeth, and she rummaged in a drawer to find an old T-shirt with a silkscreen of a mountain and sun on it that I could use to sleep in. We would, she assured me, handing over the shirt, visit my apartment the next day after breakfast to pack for the train trip, and then I could finally get some of my things. We were in the bathroom then, and she was perched on the edge of the tub, looking at me intently when she said it, her eyes filled with sympathy, but I was washing my hands with her fresh-scented lemon verbena soap, resting it carefully back in the soap dish shaped like a dinghy, and her words didn't fill me with any particular relief or solace; what was so very important to me in the apartment anyway? My ties to the things over there felt as delicate as spiderweb filament now. All I wanted was my babysitter's butterfly lamp, and her lemon verbena soap, and even her spare toothbrush, which was several times softer and cleaner than my own.

We returned to the living room area, and she tugged pillowcases over couch pillows and piled me high with a slippery green chenille blanket.

"Comfortable?"

"Very."

"Should I leave the butterfly lamp on?"

"Please."

Beneath its spill of golden light, she sat on the edge of the sofa and read me a story about a ragtag spaceship that she said she was considering for her class. "Do you think they'll like it?" "I do." "Good," she said, nodding, "good." She brought me a glass of water. She didn't seem to know what to do with me at that point, so she patted my arm, wished me sweet dreams, and then disappeared into the bathroom. It was still light outside, so the room glowed a faint blue with evening, a light rain tapping on the rooftop, and from time to time the building's pipes released and sighed. I did not move. I felt myself a broken jewel inside a jewel box. Somewhere across town, through the network of streets, my mother was in some kind of institutional building, a hospital, surrounded by doctors and the staccato voices of medical care that I'd heard through the speaker when my aunt had talked to her during earlier incidents on the phone. I lay on the couch and thought of her and did not think of her; she was central to my every thought, running underneath everything in a hum, and also erased, excised from the moment like she had never been my mother in the first place.

After a while, the babysitter exited the bathroom in some kind of pajama outfit and climbed the ladder to her own bed, where she turned pages for a long time under the brassy light of a clip-on reading lamp.

Through the windows, the blueness deepened and darkened. Silkscreens of red-gold butterflies appeared to fly around the perimeter of the lamp.

"Good night, sweet Francie," the babysitter whispered, later, clicking off her light.

She turned on her side. I could hear as her breathing slowed, and the room emptied of its other awake mind. Just me and the golden lamp. Black night outside. Something suspending. I remember this so well. How time seemed to stretch like taffy, dark nighttime taffy, made and pulled from the fabric of the sleeping and the sleepless. How tensions gathered in corners in murky clusters, and I could see them clearly from where I lay tucked into and half-held by the slippery chenille, darkness laid upon the dark, braids of muscular shadow folding slowly together. Like I was, for a second, witnessing something private and impassive about the inner workings of the world.

About a week earlier, at the parallel bedtime, my mother had done a load of laundry, and like the babysitter, had pulled fresh pillowcases over the pillows. Like the babysitter, she brought a glass of water to my bedside, and read me a story, **The Velveteen Rabbit,** one of her favorites. The sky dimmed outside. I had brushed my teeth; I had washed my face.

At the end of the story, the rabbit hopped off to eat the grass, real grass, and my mother sighed with pleasure, kissing my forehead as she stood.

"I could never leave my stuffed animals facedown," she told me. She glanced at the ground and picked up one of my teddy bears that had fallen to the floor, placing it faceup on my pillow. "How I feared they would suffocate!"

I watched her closely. She pulled covers to my chin.

"Sleep well, little Francie," she said. "Bear will be with you all night long."

She began to move about the room. This was about a week or so before she smashed her hand, and at that moment, for the last phase while I lived with her, her medication was largely in a phase of elegant titration, and despite the tape recorders in every room hidden beneath their white paper tents, we'd had a very good stretch of months. We'd been playing lots of card games. The living room walls were covered in drawings of castles we'd made together. She was enthusiastic and happy about almost every single thing I did. That night, she was wearing a new calico dress from Goodwill that suited her, with a long and floaty peasant skirt, her hair piled high upon her head like a woman from another era, secured in place by a kabob skewer. As I watched, she took her time reaching down and picking up all the various animals strewn on the floor, settling them into place on the rocking chair in the corner. She set the stuffed bear in the lap of the stuffed spaniel. She hung the stuffed monkey over the back of the chair rungs, linked by Velcro hands. She nestled the stuffed lions into a heap. It was such a comfort to see her attend to a category.

"Night-light, Francie?" she asked at the door, by the light switch.

"No, thank you."

"You sure?"

"Sure."

"Do you want any more animals with you in bed?"

"No."

"You have your special blanket?"

"I can't find it."

"Really? Where was it last?"

"I think I maybe left it somewhere."

"Oh no! Do you know where?"

"Esther's."

"Should I call her? I can easily call her—"

"No. I'll tell her at school tomorrow."

"Really?"

"Yes."

"Okay. If you're sure. I'd be happy to call. Just come get me if you can't sleep and you want me to, okay? Or anything else at all. You promise?"

"I promise."

"I tell you, I've never even heard of a child who liked the dark. You really like it?"

"Yes."

"It doesn't scare you? You don't see monsters and things in it, in the shapes of things?"

"No."

"Did I just ruin it for you?"

"No."

"You hug Bear tight if you need to, okay?"

"Okay."

"Nothing's going to hurt you, honey."

"Okay."

"Good night, darling. I love you."

"Good night."

Her face, at the light switch, shrunk into itself for a second, like an anemone poked by a finger.

When the overhead light went out and the door closed, she left me in darkness, lines of light drawn by the outside lampposts forming squares around the window shades. There were three important steps I needed to do. First, I moved my arms and legs up and down until Bear rolled off the pillow and returned to the carpet. Then, slipping out of bed softly, so soft on my toes, I reached the rocking chair in the dark, where it took only a few pushes for all those animals to tumble back to the floor, too. Finally, over to the door, where I very, very quietly turned the knob lock to horizontal.

It was a highly specific and memorable sensation, that turn. You might even say I waited all day for it. Testing the doorknob, and finding it tight. Jiggling it just to be sure. As the bolt slid into place inside the wall, everything else seemed to melt a little, and the room began to open and flow around me. The darkness lithe, even liquidy. Every day, this was the one time when I could feel myself loosen inside, not need to account for and check on my own clear outline in the world so many times over and over again. When the walls could become my delineation instead. A night-light would've only punctured things; even Bear was an irritant, when I preferred just my arms and legs to flap through the vast planes of sheets.

Far away, in the planet of the living room, I could hear my mother pressing buttons on the phone.

"Hey," she said, "it's me. Do you have a minute?"

The grays in my room began to sort into a color scale and I tiptoed back to the hulking storm-colored bed and climbed inside. It had been a good day at school. We had started working on color wheels.

"Thanks," said Mom.

She lowered her voice, but the darkness worked as an amplifier and I could hear her well. She spoke first about her day, with a few cursory words toward her ever-present search for work, and a minute or two asking my aunt about herself.

"Good, good," she said.

Then, a weighty silence.

"I know it's small," she said, "but it's just she has no special animal she sleeps with, no blanket or anything. She left her beloved blanket at a friend's house but she doesn't even seem to care. Don't you think that's strange? Even just a little? Shouldn't I worry?"

I paused, in the bed. Stopped stretching around so that I could hear her better. It wasn't that I particularly cared about the blanket issue; I did, a little, but what I was noticing right then, what unsettled me much more, was that her voice was starting to cut a slight edge. It was barely anything, so subtle most people would only find it to be animated, but containing the millimeter of tonal difference that I was recognizing right then as a gateway.

"There's something cold in her, don't you think?" Mom said. "Is there?"

Was Minn hearing it too? Minn, on the other line, the only other person in the world equally attuned to these changes?

"Okay," said my mother, after a minute. "You're right. Okay."

The medications, as they always did for her, would begin to tip out of their working order, the same way a top will ride so smoothly on its point and spin and spin like it could spin forever. My mother's wobbling began slowly too, with daily room rearranging, and constantly fidgety hands, and then she'd start writing long urgent lists in notebooks of words I could no longer decipher, or she'd check the tape recorders repeatedly, making sure they were running, or after meals she'd ask to look in my mouth: "Open up," a firm hand under my chin, like I was hoarding the food, like I had tucked a jewel under my tongue, a computer chip. She'd call me over and ask if I was real. She'd hand to me, as had so impressed Vicky, half-empty jars of pickles or mustard to give to my friends for their birthday parties.

Usually, Minn would hear the shift, too, even on the phone, and it would cue her to call up the doctors and get my mother in, and at first Mom's medication adjustments would be too extreme and she would come home and sleep all the time, and I would go stare at her in her room sleeping, this captured thing, her body changing with weight and fluid retention, the clothes from Goodwill no longer fitting, back to Goodwill for a new round of larger sizes, Aunt Minn flying up to chaperone and buying me a scone at the coffee shop to distract me and explain things to me while my mother wept in front of the mirrors at the stretched new shape of her body. At the last round of this, well over a year ago, my aunt had just had another miscarriage, and had arrived pale, shoulders drawn, sad, and my mother had tried to soothe her but her thinking was muddy and she could not figure out what to say. "For the baby," she had said, putting her hand on her sister's shoulder, her eyes hunting, dredging for context. We were back at Goodwill then, after visits to the doctor, shopping the racks. "I'll be your kid," I remember telling Aunt Minn, when my mother went off to the dressing rooms with piles of clothing folded on her arm. My aunt didn't shift her gaze. "Just kidding!" I said.

Inside my bedroom, in the pour of darkness, I kept my ears as alert as I could, but my mother was quiet as Minn spoke on the other side of the line. She was so quiet, in fact, that it was my picture of her that clarified, as if I was right there in the room, and I could vividly see my mother sitting on the stool, her skirt draping, the heel of her hand pressing into her forehead, the other hand perhaps beginning to draw lines in the telephone notebook nearby. One foot wrapped around the stool leg. The phone pressed to her ear with her shoulder. For a second, I could hold it all in my mind, but just as quickly the clarity began to fuzz, the image of her body beginning to crackle away, her and the things around her dispersing and evaporating, everything except the sharp metal skewer in her hair. Stuck in her hair, that remarkable hair, auburn and thick with waves, she a woman who was stopped on the street not irregularly and asked if she would be willing to donate a wig. Until that moment, I had seen it but not seen it. It was the minuscule shift in her voice that led me to recognize the skewer as something more than just a witty hairpin.

I got out of bed and unlocked the door.

"Mommy?" I said.

"She's here, hang on—" She turned to me. Her eyes were wet, and even bigger than usual. I could see it in her face now, too, the beginning of the turn, the slight lack of focus in her features, as if they no longer had a uniting principle of face.

We'd had a long run, I remember thinking.

"I'm scared, Mommy."

"I have to go, Minn. Francie's scared. What's wrong, honey? Did you see something? Do you want me to call about Blanket?"

"No. Put your hair down," I said.

"My hair?"

"I want it down," I said. "Please. Will you brush it on my face?"

She blinked at me, and then pulled out the skewer and there it was, tumbling, radiant, the healthiest part of her.

"Wash my face with it like you do sometimes," I said.

She laughed with relief. Me, just a needy little kid. She lifted her hair up and let it fall over my face, and it smelled of citrus and sweat and I let it mother me, that hair, all the while acutely, even coldly, aware of her hand as she let the skewer roll out of it and onto the kitchen counter next to a crusty sandwich plate left over from lunch. Our faces touched.

"Under the hair curtain," she whispered.

"Mommy," I said.

"Yes?"

"I don't like it when you put your hair high up," I said.

"You don't?"

"It scares me."

"It does? I don't have to do it. I'll never do it again."

"Don't do it," I said. "Then I can go to sleep."

"Do you want the light on? I have that nice purple and silver Saturn night-light—"

"No."

She rarely did the dishes before bed, so whatever was on the counter would likely stay on the counter until some other later unknown moment of cleaning energy, giving me enough time to pocket it in the morning and put it high in the closet, as I had done already with some of the sharper knives, wrapping them in T-shirts I had outgrown. It wasn't ever clear that she would do something with the knives, but she talked about it sometimes, how things took on a glow to her, a kind of aura, and on this day, the change in her voice was enough to spur me to action. I did not hide the hammer, which she would use to smash her hand less than a week later; I didn't think of it, and I could not put every single dangerous thing away. I could not rip out the electrical outlets and pull the wires from the walls and undo the garbage disposal. I had, one day, on a whim, brought the screwdriver to school and buried it in the recess garden, where a kindergartner had dug it up by accident and injured his thumb.

"I'll tuck you back in. It's late now, sweetie."

She walked me over, and the door to my bedroom opened onto the cave of grays but she still saw the animals right away.

"Oh, goodness! How did they all get on the floor?"

"I don't know."

"All of them? Here, let me turn on the light for a second."

"Too bright!"

"I'll be quick—"

"I was just walking around in the dark a little bit and I guess they fell off."

"Walking around, Francie? Really?"

"A little."

"You have to be careful, honey. You might bump into things. See, a night-light would really help this—"

"No night-light."

"Well. Let me settle them back, okay? Why is that shirt on your head?"

"It's too bright. Sometimes they're just on the floor when I wake up."

She paused in the middle of the room, bending

to pick up the animals. Her pretty feet, her chipped red toenails. "My father sleepwalked, you know. Maybe you do too. Oh, look at this—and Bear's over here too!"

"I'll take Bear."

In my mind: bear.

"Now, okay. All better. Lights off. We'll call Esther tomorrow, okay? Will you take the shirt off your head now, please?"

"Good night, Mommy. Thank you."

"Good night, my sweet darling."

"I love you, Mommy."

She fell into herself. "Thank you, thank you. I love you too. I love you so much."

"I can sleep now."

"You go to sleep, little person. Sweet dreams."

I dozed off shortly after, once the door was relocked, and the animals were back on the floor.

I don't know when I dozed off in the loft apartment, but it was late, much later, into the early hours of morning.

At six o'clock, an alarm sent its pellets of beeps into the darkness. Every beep pelting the warm cove of blankets like a BB gun.

"Sorry! Sorry," said a voice, "I forgot to turn it off."

The heater had clicked off hours before. The room

to which I awoke looked cold and entirely new. Some kind of blobby corner chair, wooden frames around unseeable pictures, higher walls, thin gray sunlight pearling behind floral curtains. A heavy brindled animal stretched its legs down a ladder and hopped onto my blankets.

"That's Hattie," said the voice, laughing, from above. "He's friendly. It's early. Do you want to keep sleeping?"

"No. Thank you."

The voice, a voice I knew well enough from several years of visits, worked on me like a map, and I could almost track the shift as my brain reorganized the information in the room into familiarity, pinning down the TV with the fringy scarf, the green schoolbag that I'd seen earlier leaning against a far corner, the ball bearing that was the day of the week circling through a ring of wooden time grooves into its slot: Saturday. And then there was the babysitter herself, stepping off the bottom rung of her ladder, sitting down at the edge of my bed, where Hattie traversed the bumps to settle on her leg, purring. How odd to see her up close, in her pajamas, floral pink and green, hair mussed, smiling at me, face washed clear of lipstick and daytime.

"He sleeps up in the loft; sorry, I forgot to tell you. You're not allergic to cats, are you?"

"I don't know."

"Do you feel stuffy?"

"No."

"How did you sleep?"

"He was here the whole time?"

"Asleep. He's old. He sleeps a lot. Watch, he'll have his breakfast and then climb right back up."

She scratched behind his ears.

"You look a little tired," she said, gently. "You're sure you don't want to go back to sleep?"

"No, thank you."

She stood and put a pot of coffee on in the kitchenette. Hattie jumped to the floor to rub his side against the couch edge.

"Then we are **up,**" she said. "Hey, your uncle called," looking at her phone, clicking on some buttons and listening and smiling. "They had the baby!" then playing it back to me, his excited, trembly voice: "She's here, little Victoria, she's so beautiful! Five pounds, eleven ounces. Tons of hair."

"May I have some coffee, too?"

"No, sweetie," she said, clicking it off. "It's not for kids."

"My mom gives it to me all the time," which was not true.

"Really?"

"With cream and sugar."

"You can have a sip."

Bitter, bitter.

Still, it was so much better than drowning in nighttime, this sitting with her at a kitchen table, her preparing oatmeal for me in a yellow bowl with green leaves twining around the rim, her leaning back on the counter with her hands wrapped around the warmth of a coffee mug. Hattie found his food bowl and began nosing around the kibble.

The babysitter sipped her coffee. I could feel the monster there with us, though I did not know yet what it was. I could feel it in her apartment.

"You okay?" she asked.

"The oatmeal is good."

"I'm glad. But save room, okay? We'll go to the brunch place together soon."

"Okay."

"They open at nine. We can walk. There'll be a line so it's good to get there early, but we still have tons of time and I have to shower and stuff. Do you mind if I do?"

"No."

"Then we'll go to your place and get what you need and get you packed. The train isn't until tomorrow."

"Okay."

"I have to check what time. I think ten or eleven? Something like that. Do you want to watch the lion show again while I get ready?"

"Sure."

She washed my bowl, and rinsed my bowl, and set my bowl in the drying rack. Then she washed her mug, and rinsed her mug, and set her mug in the drying rack. She saw my spoon on the table, picked up my spoon, and soaped and rinsed it, too. These actions were like manna to me, and while she showered I went to the drying rack and looked at the things in there, dripping, and the clean white bottom of her kitchen sink.

22

When I was a child, my mother read me all kinds of stories, but her favorites, and sometimes my favorites, were about things coming alive. And not just anything, but toy animals and dolls, especially, or drawings and sculptures of animals or people—specifically, objects that resembled something alive but weren't. Things poised on the supposedly porous boundary. There was no shortage of options: Corduroy the Bear riding up an escalator to find his lost button, Jack Pumpkinhead sprinkled to life by magic powder in the **Land of Oz,** figures exiting paintings in the **Harry Potter** books, Clara's nutcracker animating at midnight to take her on a journey to wonders. On a successful Saturday visit to the big Goodwill on Sixth, Mom found **Toy Story 2** on VHS for a dollar, plus a VHS player for seven more, and that afternoon she and I sat on the ratty tweed couch and laughed and laughed when Mr. Potato Head crossed the street disguised as a traffic cone.

The Velveteen Rabbit that she'd read me just the week before our split.

Pygmalion's Galatea.

Pinocchio.

But the lesson from the butterfly lamp, or the beetle paper, or the damask curtain roses, is this. It is fun to imagine in a story. It is terrifying in real life. One is a representation and one is life, and the two have nothing in common except a suggestion of group, a shared name. Pygmalion fell in love with his ivory statue, and then one day her lips grew warm and her pulse started throbbing. It is a story that has so caught the human imagination that it has been redone hundreds of times, in every art form. But it must be stated, or I must state for myself, that that is not actually possible. Statues can't come alive. Lips warm from blood, and blood needs arteries; a pulse is the satellite of a beating heart that grew from the organic structure of an embryo. We live in different worlds, the people and the objects. And I am truly not trying to state the obvious; I am working as hard as I can to explain to myself the actual size of the leap. The butterfly I found in that water glass had to gain internal functions and an external structure, had to come out of an entirely different plane of existence to make itself, but somehow it did, and what I drank down with that glass of water had a body and legs and was real, had become real. It was an active psychosis. I swallowed psychosis.

According to all the doctors I have seen, and they are not few, I am okay in the brain area. I have taken tests over the years just in case, and run on treadmills for inexplicable reasons, and have encountered the inkblots enough times that I now can anticipate the shapes. I have, because of my aunt's worry, and my mother's worry, and my own, taken the MMPI-A, the MACI, the bipolar screen, and some anxiety quizzes. I pass them all with acceptability. "I just don't see any signs," said my aunt, digging through her purse for her keys to drive us home from yet another doctor's appointment on an afternoon toward the end of my high school years after encountering the dead roses beneath the curtains at Deena's house. This was just a few days after I'd gone up to Portland by myself and sent my mother over the back of the chair, and I'd come home from Deena's house shaken, roses in my arms, a tremor in my hands, looking online right away to find a doctor who might see me, any doctor, whoever might fit, a neurologist in Glendale known for helping with unusual cases, telling my aunt in the vaguest way possible that I'd been seeing things I didn't fully understand, and would she take me, could we go. She had agreed, as she always agreed; I was in my late teens, then, and beginning to step into the true territory of risk, although my whole twenties were in question as the girls broke later than the boys.

"Your mother had all kinds of clear symptoms

at your age," she said, after the appointment, as we approached the car in the parking lot.

"She did?"

"Sure, of course, similar to what happens with her now. Pacing in the middle of the night, sleeping for twenty hours, saying certain things are talking to her. You don't do any of that."

"No."

"You're so measured, thorough. That must come from your father."

"Or you."

"Ha. I suppose that's true. Or me."

We settled into our seats, and she turned up the air conditioner and backed out of the parking space. Extracted the parking ticket from where she'd wedged it in the sun visor. Placed her credit card in the slot with precision.

Still, none of it guaranteed anything, and when I had felt, at Deena's, the familiar monstrous sensation, a feeling like something far underground was getting ready to shift and release, something I hadn't felt in years, not since my train trip south and the entrances of the butterfly and the beetle, my mind had scattered, and I'd had trouble hearing what Deena was saying about some guy at school, like she'd fallen into a tunnel, and suddenly all the things on her walls, the posters of people, the bands, the wry unicorn T-shirts, the silkscreens of reptiles, seemed dangerous, volatile. I scanned her room, looking, dreading, but it was minutes later, on our way to get a snack in her kitchen, that I passed through the living room and saw the trio of dried roses lying so benignly beneath her mother's heavy damask curtains. Those same roses, the same shade of mauve, the buds woven together exactly as the flowers intertwined in the curtain, but with brightness drained from the petals, thin and leathery from desiccation. There they were, resting on the rug. I picked them up with shaking fingers.

"What's that?" said Deena, dipping a pretzel stick into a vat of peanut butter.

23

"Do you ever hear voices?" "No." "Do you ever think anyone is following you?" "No." "Do you ever think thoughts have been implanted in your mind?" "No, no. Really. It's just the roses." "Is there a history of mental illness in the family?" "Yes." "Who might that be?" "My mother." "And your father?" "Unknown." "Can you recall any other moments where you have seen a vision like what you described?" "There have been no other moments except the ones I just mentioned. And it wasn't a vision. My friend Deena saw them too." "The roses?" "Yes." "What did she think they were from?" "She had no idea. She was very surprised. Her family hates dried roses." "You don't happen to have them here?" "I do." "They look like regular dried roses." "They are regular dried roses. Except they are made out of nothing." "And explain again how you know this?" "They were under the curtains." "But surely someone might have just accidentally dropped dried roses under the curtains?" "Except Deena was shocked, too." "Just by the presence of dried roses in her house?" "Yes." "They dislike dried roses that much?" "They really do." "Well, okay. Fine. Explain it more to me, then—what you think is that somehow the embroidered roses came to life and dropped out of the curtain and onto the floor and became dried roses?" "Yes." "And when was your mother's first psychotic break?" "She was seventeen." "And you are?" "Seventeen." "But you seem to understand that curtains cannot make roses?" "I do." "Did you see the roses emerge from the curtains?" "No, no, not at all. I've never seen that part. They were just there on the floor when I walked by." "So what do you make of it?" "Me? What do I make of it? That's why I'm here." "And your brain scan and testing all look fine." "They've always looked fine." "But then, Frann—" "Francie." "Francie. Have you ever seen a psychotherapist?" "Yes." "And?" "It's not a metaphor." "You mean the roses?" "Right. The roses are not a metaphor." "But did it help?" "It just wasn't enough." "I understand. But I have to admit, I'm finding myself a little confused. If you don't think this comes from your own mind, and you believe you're witnessing some sort of phenomenon, and you aren't demonstrating any other symptoms, why make an appointment with a neurologist?" "Who else am I supposed to see?" "To implicate the world in its own rupture?" "Exactly!" "I have no idea." "And also, Doctor, to your earlier point—" "A priest?" "—if it was just a casual drop at Deena's, why would they match the curtain exactly? As in exactly, except dead? And what about the butterfly? And the beetle?" "Or a shaman? Some kind of transcendental monk?" "Are you making fun of me?" "Sorry. Just trying to brainstorm. Do you know how much time passed between each incident?" "The roses were two days ago. The beetle was a day after the butterfly, which was ten years ago." "And were there any corresponding events in your life at these times?" "Excuse me?" "Were there any events in your life around the time of each incident that might connect?" "Why would that be relevant? It's not just about me." "Is it happening to someone else?" "Isn't it?" "Francie? Have you heard of anyone else talking about anything remotely like this?" "I mean, the only thing—" "Yes?" "Just my mother not doing well, and me upsetting her, and her not being able to take care of me. It's not really viable data." "But has that happened each time?" "Possibly." "Possibly?" "The butterfly, yes. The beetle was basically at the same time, so yes. The roses just happened." "And?" "And what?" "And, how is your mother doing?" "She left her facility a few weeks ago and tried to get her own apartment to see if she could take me back." "Did she succeed?" "She did not." "Is she doing okay now?" "We had a bad visit. But I don't see that there's any clear link to any of that." "What happened with the visit?" "I sent her over the back of a chair." "You pushed her?" "No, no, I was talking to her about all of this stuff.

About the butterfly. It was dumb. She tipped herself over." "She's all right?" "Physically, yes. Otherwise, improving." "And you were really going to move back up there?" "I had no plans to go." "Well, it seems notable, doesn't it? All these events, around the same times?" "Not to me." "There may not be a link, but—" "You're just making random guesses." "I'm just trying to gather information, Francie. Looking for patterns." "But what could the patterns possibly be?" "Well, I'm not sure. Let's review again for a moment. We'll try another angle. What was the order again here? Butterfly, beetle, roses? Butterfly first?" "Yes?" "Beetle on the train?" "Two days after the butterfly." "Roses just this week." "Yes." "So. Whatever may be happening, Francie, whatever this may be, one might also wonder if you are progressing from the entomological world into the botanical." "Doctor?" "There haven't been other categories, have there?" "What do you mean, 'categories'?" "Such as rodents? Mammalia?" "Why do you keep treating this like it's a real thing?" "Perhaps, Francie, the power is fading." "It's not a power." "Perhaps, Francie, the incidents are fading." "But they can't be real incidents." "Francie? Didn't you just say that your friend Deena saw the roses too, and that you truly believe they came from the curtains?" "But they can't **actually** come from the curtains, can they, Doctor?" "Francie? Are we even having the same conversation here?" "I just don't understand how any of this can happen."

The Butterfly Lampshade

"They're all dead?" "Excuse me?" "The things you find. They're all dead?" "Yes." "And are they dead in the picture?" "No." "The roses in the curtain—?" "Are stitchings of alive, blossoming roses." "And the beetle?" "Was from an illustration of a stag beetle walking on a twig for a grade school test." "And the beetle you found was dead?" "Rigid as a rock." "Well, that's interesting." "Yeah. I've wondered about that, too." "What do you make of it?" "I don't know. What do you make of it?" "I don't know." "It's sad, when you think about it." "Because . . . ?" "Just to make that leap all the way into the living world, to make this miraculous leap, and then, blam." "Does seem like a waste of a good miracle, doesn't it." "That first time, when I found the butterfly in the water glass, I actually thought it must've come alive and flown off the lamp only to somehow fall and drown in a water glass—" "That's where you found it? In a water glass?" "Yes." "Did you drink it?" ". . . yes . . . ?" "Just a hunch. Did you eat the beetle?" "Disgusting. No." "Go on." "That's it. Just that at first I thought the butterfly was alive for a little while, and then died. But now I think that's wrong. They're all dead. They arrive dead." "It's consistent." "It certainly is. But, Doctor, what is the 'it'?" "I guess that's the million-dollar question, isn't it?" "I guess so."

24

The tent has now bleached from the weeks and weeks in the sun. I've placed an old pillow in the back, another to sit on. There's a little trash can I empty daily in case I bring in a snack. The hand fan cost seven dollars.

My days now revolve largely around the two tasks: make a living for myself by finding and mailing the objects, and remember that time. Remember it more. Re-remember. Find another detail. Look again. There's no formal routine, so once I've awoken in the darkness and settled into my spot, I usually begin by recalling what I was thinking about the day before, trying to walk myself back into it, to mentally draw it as closely and with as much detail as I can, to include myself in it, to experience more fully. It's okay, I have told myself, to go back over the same material. It's okay to remember new times, new days. To speak it aloud formally, like a speech. To ask myself questions, like an interview. Still, it is difficult work. My mind wanders constantly. Scraps of old action TV episodes rear up out of nowhere. I make menus for lunch, or recite facts from high school government class. Song lyric intrusions. Waves of sleepiness. When I am able to focus, since I was so cut off from what was happening as a child, sometimes it is more than anything like walking myself through a blankness, and all I can do is try to measure the quality of the blankness, if it's a fizzy blank, or a misty blank, or a fog blank, or a morgue.

But even with all that, for a lot of the time, there's actually plenty to sort through. What Vicky, in her disbelief, may not understand is that even though I was barely aware of what was going on at that time, even though I was drifting through the events like some sort of person-ghost, it's not like the whole self just turns off and floats into air; we always do some sort of compensation, and for me, my entire sensory set of equipment was on high alert even as the rest of me, the processing part, closed down. I felt no feeling, and at any time of day would burst into tears severed from sadness, a physical racked sobbing like my body had to wrench it out even if my mind could not, and I'd sit like a stone during tearjerker movies, and my mother's wavery, tentative phone calls, but I can still tell you in extensive detail about the tight brown-and-beige weave of the cushion on the sofa in the principal's office waiting room as I sat looking at the secretary's rose-stoned ring on her hand with its raised central vein right before she, the principal, called me into her egg-salad-scented office with the peppery sound of jackhammers working outside to tell me behind those thick black plastic framed glasses that my uncle was flying in to take me away.

So, most of the time, there's all that to deal with. When I'm done for the morning, I crawl out, zip it up as per the usual, and close and lock the glass balcony door.

For the paying work, my job is much clearer. The new tissue paper/packing area is working well, and I've gotten faster at the time from sale to doorstep. The weekend's packed with the yard sale visits, and the week filled with activities such as post office trips, emailing back clients, photographing and keeping track of the goods, wrapping and addressing the boxes. The rusted trumpet that to one person has lost its allure or perhaps is tainted by death or disappointment is a fresh object of love and music for Edna in Knoxville, or Franklin in Alhambra, and I spend my yard sale tours trying my best to see these things that others pass by, to spot an object on a table that has lost all connection to its identity, or maybe a better way to say it is that it has been so flooded with someone else's identity that it has entirely lost its own. This might include old framed pictures, or mountains of snarled jewelry, or half-used perfume, or a shirt that doesn't look interesting in a pile, seems overworn, used, tired, spent, but once washed and ironed will flatter a woman's neckline and suddenly become the favorite new selection of her closet. These are the items to grab, to get for extremely low prices and later, large markups. And there is no shortage. The world is filling faster with those kinds of dead objects than practically anything else. I want to empty them of their former layers and hopes, and I can; all I do is buy them, and if need be, wash them, but mostly just **see** them by the acts of purchase, and documentation. Then I put their fresh new photos online, and the cycle begins again. My own apartment remains extremely spare.

25

"It's totally a cocoon," Vicky says, visiting one Saturday morning, staring at the tent. "You are in some kind of homemade cocoon bizarre thing." She has her hammer out, fixing one of the sides, which, earlier in the week, started to unpeel from the framework.

"Maybe."

"Well, that's how I'm going to think of it," she says. "Otherwise Mom still will not stop about how worried she is that you're going to jump off the balcony or something."

"She says that?"

"She just doesn't understand what you're doing. Remember how you were so determined to have a balcony? She keeps talking about that. Like, why did Francie want a balcony so much? Why did Francie quit her job? Are you sure she's being safe? Like that."

She attaches the canvas to its wooden brace and neatens it up, while I stand to the side, holding the toolkit. I surely could have fixed it myself, but I am skittish around hammers in general, and she happened to have the morning free. They've just started rehearsals for **Our Town,** and she said she's trying out different lighting cues, establishing the varying levels of blue. Is upstage pale blue more deathlike because of the suggestion of white light? Is deep blue better because the actors disappear into the darkness? The production will open in a couple months, before Thanksgiving.

"It's not like I really understand it either," I say, holding the fabric in place for her. "Does it at least get you off the hook a little bit?"

Nail in mouth: "You mean with her worrying?"

"Yeah."

"A little. Should I worry?"

She pauses, hammer up.

"No," I say.

Vicky drives the nail into the right spot, adds another for reinforcement. Earlier in the week, when the canvas panel peeled open, I found it almost impossible to concentrate with that open section letting in a triangular spot of brightness. Like a constant interrupting voice of light. I have grown accustomed to the soft filtered sun as experienced through the canvas, and also to the effect of the cave. The entire tent enterprise might even fail with a hole, because although on some level I do understand that memories are not tangible, it also seems in a very small way possible that without containment, everything I am thinking about might just stream out of me and into the city itself, never to be found again.

"Can you check one paragraph really fast before I go?" Vicky says, tucking her tools away, latching the kit. "I changed some of the wording. I cut out nice. I changed lucky to fortunate."

"Good," I say, going to grab a pen. "That sounds good. And really, I'm okay. You can tell Aunt Minn I'm not going to jump off any balcony. That is not my worry at all."

"You promise?"

"Promise."

26

I walk her to her car, Aunt Minn's car, and the backseat is piled high with costumes that she said she is washing early so they can alter them for the show. One of them seems too princely for **Our Town,** with a slip of velvet on the collar, but she says there's a way to cover it with cotton and make it look more like a janitor for the Stage Manager's role. I thank her again, and hug her, and as she's settling into the driver's seat, the building manager with the gray ponytail walks through the parking lot, heading toward the mailboxes, and when she sees me, she stops. "Hey, what's that thing on your balcony?" she calls over, her hands full of letters, all stamped and ready to travel the country. "That orange thing you put up? Is that safe?" "Oh, it's just this tent thing," I call back. "Nothing to worry about." "You're not sleeping out there, are you?" She peers through the windshield at Vicky, who waves. "No, no, not at all," I say. "Because," the building manager adds, flapping the letters, "it's not up to code for sleeping. The balcony is not zoned for sleeping." She squints her eyes at us for a moment, and then heads over to the mailbox, and when I lean back down, Vicky is raising her eyebrows, turning on the car. "Everybody worrying about you, Francie," she says, shaking her head, and I watch as she navigates into the flow of traffic, how she changes lanes so smoothly, the signaling, the brake lights. The building manager and I walk back up the stairs together; we're on the same level, a few doors apart, and she is sorting through a pile of rent envelopes now, retrieved from the mailbox. I can see mine in the stack. It's dark, and the moths are fluttering to the lights on the outside hallways, plastering their bodies to the plastic shields. "I just like to know what's going on," the building manager says, glancing up, hand on her doorknob. "You wouldn't believe the kind of stuff that goes on in these buildings. Good night," she says, disappearing into her apartment. "Good night."

27

The brunch place was crowded. I plowed through my stack of marionberry pancakes. The babysitter drank three cups of coffee. Afterward, we walked a few busy blocks down Burnside to a temporary craft museum for kids, where I sat at a table and strung faceted beads on a wire, and when I felt the tears rising to the surface as they seemed to do every few hours, like my body needed to wring them out the way one might do with a drenched washcloth, she found an outside bench in a patch of sunlight and smoothed my hair as I wept. A friend of hers joined us for a little while: Terry, with the dark curls and cream-colored scarf. They sat close together, whispering, and while they spoke, I drew light patterns inside, in what they called the luminosity room, a closet-like space where I could wield a fiber-optic hose that drew streaks of red on the wall like a murder made of light that washed away in seconds without a trace. I did it over and over again. The babysitter put in a call to my uncle, who said my mother was eating and drinking but still wasn't ready to talk on the phone, but that the baby was doing well. They would be bringing her home the following day. Wait, my mother? No, no, sorry. The baby. She was eating also. She had pooped.

Terry kissed the babysitter on the cheek and waved goodbye.

We walked together along the riverbank. We lay on the grass and looked at the clouds.

Throughout the day, if pressed, I might say I felt, even then, something waiting for me back in the babysitter's apartment. I felt it tugging at me, and I feared it a little but also welcomed it, because although it did not seem entirely safe, it was also, without question, mine. In this way my attention on that day was split into three equal parts: one part riding steady with my mother in the hospital, connected to her even though I could not picture her so joined to a void in which she levitated in white space like a floating corpse magician. Then, a focus upon the activity at hand, which was for a while drawing untraceable murders with a red-light hose, while wondering vaguely if Terry might be the babysitter's girlfriend. Finally, the tug to the thing in her apartment, which had not yet formed. I remember this all clearly. When the babysitter and I went to a diner and had cheeseburgers and fries and milkshakes, and laughed a little about the red straws in the shakes and how tall they were, like superstraws, the three separate pulls maintained like split roads inside me driving to different directions at the same time: mother awareness, dinner restaurant straw activity, babysitter's apartment tug. After dinner we went briefly to my own apartment to get a few of my things, including the tape recorders and the brown bunny and the word searches. That part we rushed through; I did not want to stay long. It had been only a day and a half but with the dishes crusting in the sink and the trace scent of my mother's gardenia mist and the bedroom doors left open like the people had atomized, it all felt like the wreckage of another life, which it was.

On the kitchen counter rested a hammer, and the cordless phone lolling on its back.

Finally, a walk back to the babysitter's loft where after washing up she tucked me again under the chenille as I fell asleep fast for night number two, living and dreaming of the tug, at the site of the tug, inside it. I didn't hear her mount the ladder, or settle into her blankets, didn't see her turn off her light that time, but still, inside the restlessness of sleep, the tug stayed with me, dragging things to the surface, rumbling in the corners, filling my dreams with motion.

28

Shortly after my aunt and uncle had welcomed me into their house, Aunt Minn pulled a stool over to her desk in her bedroom and asked me to come shop with her at the computer. Vicky, who could now hold her head up, was in a cotton backpack strapped to her chest, facing out, babbling, but Aunt Minn was able to position her hands in such a way that she could type.

It was early June, late in the morning, and you could already feel the intensity of the Santa Ana heat wave pressing against the windows. From what my aunt and uncle had told me at meals, all of us sitting together around the circular table in the windowed nook of their cheerful butter-colored kitchen, this was just the beginning of what was likely to be an exceedingly hot summer. Burbank was known to break the hundred-degree mark on many days from July to October. "No marine layer here," Uncle Stan said, smiling, drinking his passionfruit iced tea with unmistakable pride.

The Butterfly Lampshade

I hovered in their bedroom doorframe. I still found it difficult to cross doorways into rooms in their house without explicit invitation.

"Come in, Francie, come!" Aunt Minn patted the stool. "Please."

Her desk was positioned by a large window that overlooked their backyard, a lawn of radiant green with an apricot tree and a robust plum and a series of terra-cotta pots growing thick-petaled black rose succulents and some kind of orange land coral. My aunt and uncle were not, as far as I could tell, richy-rich, but due to the sprawl of Southern California, land in the valley was far less expensive than in the city proper, or in Portland, and my mother's and my apartment could've dropped from the sky and fit into their yard alone. Inside their bedroom, curtains flowed gauzily from silver rods, lifting with the rare breeze to flutter toward the sky-colored bedspread, the crystal knobs, the puffed and quilted chair.

I settled onto the stool, and Aunt Minn clicked on an everything store full of pictures and prices where we bought me new shorts, a T-shirt with a hen on it, and a red baseball cap for those upcoming scorching summer days. "What are summers like in Portland?" she asked, and I told her I wore shorts there, too. That I wore sunscreen, even hats. She picked out a pillow she liked with stitched stars for my bed, and then typed in **lamp** and brought us to the lighting section. I had been living there for only a few months by that point, and the butterfly's emergence was still shockingly fresh in my memory, was something I thought about all the time, and seeing rows of any kind of decorated lampshade startled me.

"You shouldn't have to read with a flashlight for the rest of your life," Aunt Minn laughed. She kissed the top of Vicky's fuzzed head. "I'm sorry about that."

"I don't mind."

"Kids use flashlights to cheat on the lamp," she said. "You can't sneak if it's your only option!"

"I don't need to sneak."

"Here, look," she said. "What do you think?" The screen had broken into many squares, and inside each square was a different lampshade.

"Do you like horses?" She navigated the page swiftly, clicking on the horse example, where chestnut thoroughbreds ran around the perimeter.

"No, thank you."

On her desk, the glass cube of caught flowers weighed down stacks of bills, a lumpy clay blob held an assortment of pens, and I read, for what would be the first time, the sign above her computer on its hammered piece of white tin that stated, in soft cursive, **Slow Down**.

"Why slow down?"

She followed my gaze. "Oh, I just go too fast," she said. "Too much to do every minute. Angels?"

"No angels, please," I said.

"Ladybugs?"

I pointed to a lampshade in the bottom corner.

"Clouds and rainbows?"

"Clouds and rainbows are good," I said.

"Or, pears?"

"Better clouds and rainbows," I said.

"Then that's what it will be!"

She clicked a few more times, and ran her lips over the baby again.

"What is that?" I asked, pointing now to the baby's head.

The skin was pulsing right at the top of it. I had seen it since arriving, many times, all the time, but had never found the right moment to ask.

"Ah," said Aunt Minn, resting her cheek near it. "That's called the fontanelle. Where her skull hasn't fully grown together yet. That's her heartbeat you're seeing. Intense, isn't it?"

I nodded, vaguely. The skin looked dented, broken.

"What's under the skull?"

"Her brain."

"Oh."

Aunt Minn did some more clicking on the computer, inputting her credit card number and address. While she did, as a private internal activity, I pictured myself walking over and carefully selecting one of the ballpoint pens from the lumpy clay holder on the other end of the desk, and then returning to her chair to plunge it directly into Vicky.

I did not deliberately imagine this kind of thing happening. It rose up on its own, like a little secret movie intrusion, and it had been happening—this imagining—for weeks. Knives and fire into the babysitter, sharp pointed items into Vicky. I'd arrived at the house with the thoughts already inside me, but the presence of a baby and her absurd helplessness had made it all so very much worse. Every room I walked through in Burbank contained possible, tempting weaponry: earring back, fork, pencil, paper clip. The pearl letter opener Uncle Stan displayed on his desk, the plentiful wooden block of knives on the kitchen counter. I did not understand why I kept thoughts like these so close to the surface—I knew I loved the babysitter, and as far as I could tell, I didn't particularly want to hurt the baby; I liked the baby well enough, enjoyed making her smile at me, enjoyed the way her toes wiggled and her legs kicked, but I still couldn't help picturing it, mating the sharp object to the soft area.

As long as Aunt Minn or Uncle Stan or some other adult was close by, the likelihood of me doing anything seemed small, but I did not trust myself at night, when the adults were asleep, and shortly after moving in, due to nightmares and an almost constant preoccupation with the state of my hands, had asked my aunt to install that lock on my bedroom door, the lock that had inspired Vicky's personal essay though she had never understood its original purpose. At first, Aunt Minn misunderstood and bought me a brass model that locked from the inside, like it had been in Portland, wanting very much to respect my privacy, and to replicate what I'd had at my previous home, so I had to explain through a fountain of tears that I wanted a lock on the **outside** this time, so that while it was nighttime I could not get out. That I wanted to be bolted **in**. It had taken many go-arounds before she, extremely reluctantly, agreed. "Just in case I sleepwalk outside and hurt myself, like Grandpa did," I had begged her, though I had never sleepwalked in my life.

"How is everything going so far?" Aunt Minn said, at the computer, finalizing her purchases and swiveling to face me. "I mean—" She blushed. "I know it can't be easy—"

"It's nice here," I said.

"You're so quiet and easy. You can ask for things."

"I don't need anything."

"A bike? We'll get you a bike."

"Sure. Thank you."

"I used to love clouds and rainbows too."

"They're very pretty."

"We could have a painter come and paint some clouds and rainbows on your walls—would you like that? I have a friend who loves to do things like that; she's good, too. Let's do it! Okay?"

"Okay."

She looked at me closely, smiling, hopeful, with her protruding collarbone and concerned eyebrows. She exercised too often, it seemed, and wore her wool cardigans even on warm days, and I often saw the point of her jaw tensing as she grinded her teeth, but her eyes, small, alert, always felt caring to me.

"Would you like to hold her, honey?"

"No, thank you."

29

These were not isolated imaginings, either; also, around that time, I had been courting and circling yet another sharp object, this one based at the home with my mother.

After she had removed the kabob skewer from her hair, leaving it on the counter while we slept, I had woken extra early the next morning, unlocked my door, tiptoed into the kitchen, and taken it to hide as planned on a high shelf in the closet. My mother was still sleeping, and did not wake up, or check to see what I was doing, and in the subsequent days, we had our meals, and played our card games, and she never asked if I'd seen where her clever hairpin had gone off to. But a few days later, while staring out a school window as an older grade kicked a soccer ball around the emerald green field, the one who seemed preoccupied with the kabob skewer turned out to be me, as I found myself firmly fixed to the thought that the skewer might be of some use to me, might serve some of my own project purposes, and that maybe I could just borrow it for a brief moment that afternoon. This ended up being just a day or so before my mother shattered her hand with a hammer.

We were home together that day after school, my mother and I, an overcast and rheumy afternoon with fat drips falling off the eaves from a noontime rain. The air smelled of loamy soil, and worms flipped and rolled on the sidewalk. Each day since the kabob skewer, my mother had seemed a little more revved up, a little harder to understand, and that afternoon she had picked me up at school on foot, waiting with her body in the pickup line as if she were a car, making beeping sounds from the curb which made me laugh with delight and continued unease because something about it wasn't just theatrical. She was starting to shed excess energy. I could almost see it shooting rays off her body. After our postschool puddle walk, she'd settled in to make an early dinner in the kitchen, spreading mayonnaise on bread and rolling slices of turkey. I'd done my job of ripping up some lettuce for the salad, and in as stealthy a way as I knew how, I picked up a stool and lugged it to the front hall. The closet was in the living room/entryway of the apartment, and my mother's back was to me as she rolled and rerolled the turkey slices with the kind of brittle insistence I had forgotten but was instantly recognizing upon its return. The days had been growing steadily worse. For this one, she wanted to make sure each sandwich had five slices of rolled turkey. She had told me about it on the walk home several times. Her hands couldn't stay still. They could not hold the roll, the turkey kept unfurling, and I could feel the frantic build in her, even with her back to me, even as I climbed the stool and reached my own hand up.

The closet smelled of damp wool and wet slickers from our rain walk, when she had bubbled over with laughter over our reflections in the puddles, and our neighbor walking by with his two white dogs had stared at her, smiling, and said, "You'd think it never rains here!" as she raised her face and palms to the sky like a lady in a movie. The edge, by the hour, was expanding into the whole. I reached into the darkness of the closet and groped around until I felt the skewer with my hand, my seeing, hunting hand, knowing its smooth wooden handle and pointed tip, and I brought it down and held it close by my leg, passing her muttering at the turkey rolls, me replacing the stool quietly at the kitchen counter.

Inside my room, the animals were all on the rocking chair, set in their furry zoo tableau from the previous night where once again she had put them so carefully in place with a methodical concentration I saw her use with hardly anything else. I had watched, irritated, with gritted teeth, from my outpost on the bed, though by that phase of her decline I hadn't dared knock any of them down. Still, it had all seemed such a lie, a dumb lie, a corroborated lie I right then no longer wanted to join, so I settled myself on the floor in front of Bear, bear, the bear, and using the tip of the skewer, pointed its sharp end at the animal's soft brown furry center, and broke into the cotton. I tore at the fabric until I could see the white polyester stuffing and pull it out and empty the bear as its eyes sank and its body collapsed. Something was burning in the kitchen. Alongside the turkey sandwiches, she was trying an ambitious side dish recipe, something with caramelized brussels sprouts and garlic. I ripped the bear into a pile. Then I went down the row, driving the skewer into every animal, gifts from various birthdays and holidays over the years, the monkey, the bunny, the dog, the second bear, the lion, the second lion, forcing the sharpness into their bodies, tearing into fur, throwing out fluffy interiors, seeing their forms sigh and sink. I remember feeling so energized and liberated by all of it, like it was a good plan, a useful plan, that it might help her understand what was a person and what was a toy, that possibly I was doing her a service in terms of reality, of what constituted reality, and that there was no time to lose as she tottered on the edge of not knowing. That she did not have to every night pile them into the rocking chair with so much concern and attention, that she could step on them, throw them, let them fall facedown and stay there, that they were objects, not people, that they could not suffocate because they had no lungs. I heard the fan flip on in the kitchen and the sound of water running and her crying, and when she came into my doorway holding a dishtowel, with the caustic smell behind us of burnt plastic, stepping into my room to tell me what had failed with dinner only to encounter the stuffing all over the floor, the guts spilled, the raw furred shells, her face lost all color. She opened her mouth but no words came out. I even almost thought I saw it happen, the firmness of her thinking breaking into soft disconnected pieces, the rapid acceleration of a descent already begun. I had not caused it, but I did, without question, make her worse. "Francie," she breathed, and I ran into the kitchen to see if there was anything on fire but just blackened brussels sprout boats in a pan and the remnants of a plastic spatula which had torqued into a rolling wave. She began to sob in my room, like she had known and loved all these animals, like they were her cherished pets, or friends, and I could hear her moving around the room, shifting things around on the floor and without seeing could guess and would bet that she was gathering all the stuffing and slowly pushing it back inside their cotton bodies and holding the fur closed like they were, each one of them, her mind.

Why did I do it? Why did I ever think it might be useful to her to find any stuffed animals torn to pieces, when just seeing them on the floor had overwhelmed her with fear? Did I **want** to harm her? She was so easy to harm. In the memory, in the tent, touching the canvas edges to keep me partially in the present, I was, with my eyes closed, still standing by the burned pan in the kitchen, like a murderer caught with a murder weapon, skewer in hand, surrounded by blistered garlic bits and the metallic clank of the oven fan and the sounds of my mother's anguish in the next room. It accelerated everything, this ripping of animals. I had to have known that something would tip. I held tight onto the canvas of the tent, and I remember I'd thought about returning the skewer to the shelf in the closet and tucking it as far back as I could in there, into the darkest recesses, but I could feel her fear of me flooding into the room, so I walked to the front door and opened that instead. It had started raining again, the pattering sound of raindrops on wet leaves, and I grasped the skewer's handle and hurled it as hard as I could past all three floors, clattering down the steps, tumbling into greenery. It was a real risk now to a walker or stair climber in the rain in the dark, a spear flying or poking up without warning, but just in case she was right about me, I did not want it in the house.

She stayed in my room, quiet, and I stood at the window for a long time, and watched the rain.

PART THREE

Butterfly

30

Ovid wrote the poem about the sculptor's statue coming to life. Then, Gérôme made a painting about the poem about the sculptor's statue coming to life. Everyone wants a piece of that story, to imagine this amazing transformation, but it's all still operating on the same plane, art talking about art: sculpture, poetry, painting, and on. The movie about the talking toys is still a movie, so the toys and the movie slide around in the same territory, all these pieces moving freely from art-stillness into art-life with pleasure and without stress. From this safe place, the viewer or the reader can experience Aristotle's famous concept of catharsis, where we feel things based on what is seen or read or heard, purging trapped emotions in the body. It all can happen because it is not real—the power comes from the passage of one removal (art), into another removal (person not experiencing trauma in the moment), and from this dual removal, we can be moved. Bam.

The puncture is different. This is the realm of the traversing, the psychotic event, mind traveling into thing. I can think of no more palpable definition than the instance of the man who went into a movie theater showing a movie with guns in it and, appearing to witnesses like he was dressed as one of the characters in the movie, took out real guns, shot some of the people watching, and killed them.

Did he understand they would die? Is it even possible to understand? The rupture was in his mind, governed by the damaged rules of his mind, but the event was not in his mind, and happened to actual people, who were living their lives and going about their days, and whose skin could be penetrated by the movement of his fantasy into them. No elusive interplay from art into a person's soul anymore; this was blood pouring forth, life force draining. And the witnesses, the survivors, sitting in their movie seats, what about those people? They go on with their lives, holding on to that rupture. Witnesses of horror, and witnesses of rupture.

On a small scale, a tiny scale: once, when I was very young, before the butterfly, before the beetle, I was thinking about a red crayon while playing outside for no reason I can remember when I came across a red crayon in the middle of the sidewalk. There it was, between concrete squares, pointed, red, jacketed. I remember this vividly. It was brand-new, and a perfect tomato red, and exactly like the one I'd had in my mind. The leaf blower across the street faded into silence. It was one of the most terrifying moments of my life. I bent down and picked it up and I must've been at school or near school because I remember bringing it inside, and hiding it in our giant classroom bin of crayons so I would never be able to find it again, but of course I could; I saw it every time we drew, saw it on the walls of the classroom rubbed into apples, hearts, mouths.

"I can see what you're thinking," my mother said sometimes, when she was feeling unsure, "you hate me, don't you. Honey. Do you hate me?" and I would stand there with the most expressionless face I could muster and try to recall what I had actually been thinking, because the fact of her asking had made it a little true.

31

Do you need any water, Francie?

No, thanks. I'm fine. I brought myself a glass of water.

And if you need to use the bathroom?

I already went. But just in case, I have a bucket. I found one in the garage. Is that okay?

Jesus. Are you serious? It's like a prison cell.

It's what I want.

Toilet paper?

I brought a roll in from the bathroom.

You just call if you need anything else, okay? If I don't hear you, call louder. Don't be afraid of yelling.

Okay.

I'm a very light sleeper. I'm up a lot with the baby, too.

Thank you.

And you're sure you're comfortable in there?

Yes.

You won't jump out the window or anything?

No.

Promise?

Yes.

But if there ever is a fire, then you definitely jump out the window, okay? Stan, do you think it's a burp? Will you try the arm position?

Okay.

I love you, Francie. I'm so glad you're here. We both are. Sorry we keep being so distracted. We'll talk to your mom again this weekend.

Will I be going back?

To Portland? I don't think so, honey. I'm sorry. Did you think—?

It's okay.

It's just better for you to be here right now—

Will I go back later?

I guess it's possible. But I think once you're here we want you to feel settled here. We'll go see your mother soon. We'll make a plan to visit soon.

Okay.

I know it must be so different.

It's okay.

I love you, Francie. I'm glad you're asking for what you need.

Good night, Aunt Minn. Will you do the door?

I honestly don't think I can let myself do it.

I can reach my hand around.

I don't like it, Francie.

It's okay. I like it.

Careful of your fingers. Okay. Okay. Can you hear me? How is it?

It's good.

I can unlock it for you at any time.

It's really good.

I'll be right nearby. I'm going to walk Vicky up and down this hall. Do you think she's still hungry, Stan? Sleep well, Francie. What time can I unlock you?

When you are up in the morning.

Probably around six-thirty then.

Okay.

Good night, Francie.

Good night, Aunt Minn.

Say good night, Vicky. Good night to Francie. She's waving her little hand at you.

Good night, Vicky. See you in the morning.

32

The morning after I ripped up all my stuffed animals, my mother went to the kitchen early to make breakfast. The rain had cleared, and out the windows the sky had intensified into a saturated and fervent blue. Mom was pouring cereal into bowls, and when I emerged from my room, she nodded at me as I sat down on one of the counter stools. She was quieter than usual but still spoke to me, asked how I had slept, if I wanted milk or juice. Before I left for school, I made a point of calling my friend Esther's house and leaving a message asking her to please bring my baby blanket to school, the one I had left at her house the previous week at a sleepover, where I had alienated her probably forever by pretending, in my sleeping bag, not to know who she was. "It has little sheep on it and a satiny border," I told the phone. "I would really like it back. Please." I could feel my mother's eyes on me as I called, and soon after I hung up, the button from the tape recorder on the kitchen counter clicked up, which meant she had likely pressed it to record the minute she woke up.

After I brushed my teeth and changed into school clothes, we sat together on the top of the staircase and waited for Alberta's mother to pick me up. If I squinted, I thought I might be able to see the shine of the kabob skewer below us, trapped in a bundle of wet ridged hydrangea leaves. The usual neighbor walked by with his two small white dogs. My mother was sitting an inch or two farther away from me than usual.

"What will you do today?" I asked as we stared out.

"Look for a job."

"Really?"

"Maybe. I need to get a job."

Her hands sprung around her lap. She did it low and light in her lap, as if I would not notice. She lived, we lived, off some government disability funding, money from her parents, plus money from Aunt Minn and Uncle Stan. She received three checks a month, in three different envelopes.

"I'm sorry about the toys. I don't know why I did it."

She turned to look at me. For a moment, she observed me, her eyes touring my face.

"Your face looks different," she said.

"My face?"

"Is it different?"

I shook my head, touched my cheeks. "No," I said. "I don't think so."

"It just looks a little different," she said. She smiled.

"It's me, Mommy."

"Your nose, it just looks like it's a little different this morning. Your eyes."

"It's me, Mommy. Are you feeling okay?"

She kept her smile pointed at me, but her hands continued springing. Alberta's mother drove up. She didn't like to honk, so she just waited below with the motor running, and Alberta waved at me as usual from the backseat. They had moved my booster to their car, as if I was also their child.

"They feel like my regular eyes."

For a moment, my mother's face relaxed. Her hands settled on her knees. "Of course," she said. "Of course they are. Have a good day at school, sweetie. What are you working on these days?"

"Color wheels."

"Wonderful, then. Blue with red."

"Green with purple."

Her eyes rested on the distant rooftops. "And bring back that blanket."

"I will."

33

My train to Los Angeles was scheduled to leave at two in the afternoon, and I woke up in the loft again on that Sunday in the very early hours, this time with no alarm. The babysitter was still asleep; I could hear her steady breathing, and the occasional licking sounds of Hattie grooming himself. For a long time I watched the windows change with the light, watched the room turn back into itself again, imagining there was no travel ahead, and instead a long and cozy Sunday of activities with her and me and the city together, all dappled by the scent of lemon verbena.

The order of the morning was, at first, the same as the day before: Hattie descending, then babysitter, coffee burbling, the slow stirring of oatmeal, a call to Uncle Stan, baby update, mother update, Aunt Minn recovering well, information about the steward.

By then, the light was growing fair and warm, and the babysitter had opened her curtains and shades so sun rays could move into the room to place glints into the objects and reflecting surfaces. The monster, whatever the monster feeling was, the feeling that had been growing and swelling and tugging over the last two days, had passed. It had laid its turd and moved on. I felt the freshness in the room, and despite the circumstances, and the upcoming train departure, I ate my oatmeal with brown sugar and butter happily, two bowls-full. The sunlight shared the room with us, greeting us, reaching to us, so it was just natural and participatory to let my eye locate and enjoy the various glints, the babysitter's coral-colored speckled glass vase up high on the bookshelf, the corner mirror by the door with a star of light in its top corner, and something reddish and gold glinting on the surface of the water glass by my couch bed. I finished the second bowl of oatmeal and brought it to the sink. The babysitter smiled at me as I washed the bowl and spoon and placed them on the drying rack, tucking the bowl against a wire hill, resting the spoon, pretending it was my drying rack, my daily chore, and as I did it the red-gold sparkle on the water glass occurred to me again like a pleasant thought I needed to revisit, what pretty light, what a pretty room it was on a morning touched by the gleam of a new spring sun. The babysitter rose to go use the bathroom. For a second, I thought to call out to her before she passed through that door and out of the moment, to show her the special brightness this morning had offered to us in her apartment, but for whatever reason, the impulse passed.

She entered the bathroom, and the door lock clicked. Soon, we would fold the blankets on my couch bed together into tidy squares that would return to the shelves of her closet. She would place the dry bowl and spoon back in her cabinets, and on Monday she might pass by my classroom and see my own teacher peeling my name sticker off my cubby, explaining to the other kids that I had moved away to another town. Perhaps the class would send me a letter or two. In a couple hours, the babysitter and I would take the bus together to the train station, where we would arrive early to get everything in order before I would board the train and take it a day and a half south to Los Angeles, California, the place I would soon be calling my new home. I had a sleeper car for the night portion, a "roomette." I would meet the steward, my second cousin, a kind and thoughtful chaperone.

I turned from the sink and tucked in my chair at the kitchenette table. On some level I must have known something important was happening, had happened, because I can remember filling with what I would now call a formality of movement, like adulthood was brushing through my body, a gust of adulthood moving both through me and out of me and formalizing me in its wake. I carefully sidestepped the edge of the couch and moved closer to the small table and the water glass. I smoothed back my hair and brushed my cheeks clear of sugar. Hattie lapped at the water in his bowl.

Up close, it became clear that the glint of light was more than a reflection of sunrays in the water glass but had itself shape, solidity. What had appeared to be a pool of gold revealed the body of the butterfly, with red-golden wings and splattered red dots and thin black antennae, drifting on the top of the glass of water. It was a dead real butterfly, floating on the top of the water. There were no windows open in any part of the loft. It was spring, and still too cold to leave a window open at night. The door had been locked. Butterfly migration had passed.

So, I saw it, and at first it was just itself, just the glass of water with a dead butterfly in it, an image suspended and unconnected to anything else, until my mind remembered where it had seen such a butterfly before, found the link, and linked it.

Until the most predictable and unthinkable thing in the world was to tilt my head, and look at the shade.

34

My mother's head did graze a table the moment after her birth, due to an unexpected tripping, and although the doctors assured them that the baby was fine, and although our family does have genetic links to illnesses of the mind (a great uncle, a second cousin), that bump, and the metered gulping cry afterward, the splotch of wet red on the skull of an infant, is what my grandmother saw as the source of her firstborn's illness which began rising to the surface as early as four years old. She preferred to think of it as world-imposed rather than cellular, and every year at Christmastime, she sent that doctor a bottle of poison. "You could get in a lot of legal trouble for that, you know," Aunt Minn told her, on a visit for Grandma's sixty-fifth birthday, the memory surfacing in the tent one morning out of my usual framework of times, rising up like a piece of furniture spit from the ocean, the tangible details of all of us sitting on the shaggy brown living room carpet together, radio tuned to the oldies station, wrapping holiday gifts for other people since Grandma didn't like being the center of celebration. I didn't particularly want to court this memory, but there it was, in full form, Mom in a corner, turquoise skirt hitched around her thighs, painstakingly folding shining metallic paper around a box of chocolates for the mail carrier. "Oh," Grandma said to Aunt Minn in a knowing voice, "he understands." She stood to go run cold water over a pot of hard-boiling eggs, moving with deliberation due to a formerly shattered hip, and we all stopped to watch as she left the room.

This would not turn out to be a particularly good visit. It would also be, for a brief moment, glorious. I could feel the pieces of it starting to take shape inside me, shifting in the tent as the memory expanded and sharpened, projecting myself back in that room, its gift-filled den, and while the adults finished ripping off pieces of tape, and wrapping, and Grandma and Aunt Minn peeled eggshells in the kitchen, I toured the perimeter in my mind and in the room, peering at the framed photographs on the walls. There was Mom as a baby, with her healed skull, crawling. There was Minnie beaming in a puffy pink parka. Grandma holding a stick with a marshmallow on it. Grandpa driving his favorite banana yellow car. At the time of that visit, my grandparents still lived in the same house the girls had grown up in, ten miles west of Corvallis, across the road from a fragrant copse of evergreens, and in those early photos, those very young snapshots, it is difficult to tell the daughters apart. They wave their posey arms, smile their teeth at the camera in front of the pale blue clapboard house with a large, untamed yard, a tangle of trees and creek dogwood my mother had described to me on the drive down as one of the safe places of her childhood, where she could find hiding spots under the curls of ferns and rest for long periods of time. "I'll give you a tour," she told me as we veered toward the exit ramp. "The yard part is peaceful."

The house itself, she explained, had frightened her. The walls were too whispery, the rules unclear. Grandma was always expecting things but nothing was stated outright, so my mother felt herself constantly failing and never understanding why. She heard voices in the plaster muttering that she was a bad person. She dreamt of claws ripping at her face. At night, Minnie often climbed into her bed to nestle her body against my mother's, to press a warm young relief into her, but my mother would still cry, and pull at her head, and it was at three-year-old Minn's suggestion that they drag Mom's mattress to the middle of the room, as far from the walls as possible. Later, they hauled the mattress outside, to the backyard, under the starry limitlessness of night sky, with a waterproof cover, and as an adolescent, my mother brought her boyfriends right to this mattress, during school hours or after. She had told me all this during the drive south on the highway, spilling out details, the scent of cold fir wafting in through the broken back window, morning sky clouds bundled on the horizon, but as we slowed down and moved through the residential streets, she began trailing off her sentences, and by the time she pulled the car to her parents' curb, she was silent. "I'll tell you more another time," she murmured, switching off the ignition. Years later, it was Minn who filled in more, the recessed lights in her living room dimmed to yellow coves so we didn't have to look too closely at one another, me asking on one of our sofa evenings after Vicky's bedtime what it had been like with the mattress, my aunt choosing her words slowly, carefully, explaining in a weighted voice that for understandable reasons my mother seemed to trust her body most below her head, and sometimes had sat around the backyard on that mattress nude, beautiful, supine, with her breasts open to the air, just like, said Minn, the woman in the painting **Le Déjeuner sur l'herbe** had stepped right out of the frame and into their yard. "She was so intimidating," Minn said, shaking her head, "and so in her own world," staring past the living room's walls; "I had to leave my art history class when that painting came up on a slide. I could not even bear to look at it. Do you know it?" "No." "Maybe for the best." Grandma and Grandpa, she told me, installed a black shade on the curtain that looked out onto the backyard and when Mom would come home with a companion, they just pulled the shade and turned up the TV. She was on the birth control pill as soon as possible, and they always left out a full container of condoms. "Is this too much to hear?" Aunt Minn had asked me, her voice low, glancing over. I was an adolescent myself by then, and much of the listening had been managed by the absorbing parallel activity of running the fringe of her embroidered couch pillows over the palm of my hand, trying to snag the individual strings onto my life and love lines. I shook my head. I had, in general, no functional gauge about what might constitute too much or not enough.

At Grandma's birthday weekend, my mother and I visited the rooms of the house, and found the mattress still in the backyard, leaning against a gardening hut, circled by vines, traversed by squirrels. We stood on the porch and looked at it together like tourists at a museum. I asked her if her parents had ever forced her to sleep inside. "No," she said, thoughtfully, picking damp leaves woven into the trellis. "Only on rainy days. That was good of them, wasn't it? They knew I was more stable on that mattress than hardly anywhere else. It was the mattress, or me clawing at my head." She stroked my hair. "Not that you should ever do such a thing, little Francie," she said. "You have so many more choices than I did."

I rested my head on her hip. This was a few months before our own impending split, and my mother had been, for the last year or so, on that newly titrated and wonderful cocktail of meds that had seemed to put her in order in a way I hadn't remembered happening before, like she had been decluttered internally. Weeks earlier, for Alberta's eighth birthday, we had ventured together to Goodwill and picked out a fresh-looking purple-eyed doll and she had helped me wrap it with sheets of unused golden tissue paper and clear tape and even an eyelet ribbon. While sitting by the fireplace, before Grandpa put her through his usual job grilling, she had laughed at her father's jokes with a lightness and appropriate timing that had made everyone's face lift. It had not been an entirely tense morning. It had started out like a balloon. At one point earlier, after wrapping all the gifts and peeling all the eggs, a pregnant Aunt Minn and Uncle Stan had, perhaps in response to the sweet calm in the air and some tune they recognized on the radio, moved close together, and began a modest two-step around the living room, him humming in a robust bass no one had ever heard before, her mouth soft with happy embarrassment. They had just found out the fetus was a girl. Their trying had lasted years, including regular calls to Portland with Minn weeping on the other side from the miscarriages, and my mother's voice dropping to low, and my mother sitting by the phone after hanging up looking quietly at the wall for a while, and how good it felt from the satellite of my room to hear her effectively soothe someone else. Around my grandparents' living room my aunt and uncle swayed, fizzing with joy, to a meld of big band pomp and sports announcer chat in the next room, my aunt's face quiet and glowing, and for a moment then I wished they were my parents and I that baby, which I felt uneasy remembering, because, in a way, it came true; when they'd finished dancing and went to get glasses of water, laughing, I'd walked over to where my mother was sitting on the brick step among all the wrapped presents and took her hand. She rested her cheek on my hand, tears glittering in her eyes.

I picked up the red cellophaned bottle of poison. "Will he drink it?"

She wiped her eyes and said no, no, that Grandma didn't even always send it, that it was a kind of deal between the doctor and my grandmother. "Probably he just puts it under his sink," she said, "for rats." She took the bottle from me and pointed out the label under the red cellophane with its stark white skull and crossbones. "The label is very clear, see?" she said. "It's only the cellophane that's confusing."

Minn came over to us with her glass of sparkling water, flushed and lovely from the dance, shrugging on the yellow cardigan that I would come to know as her favorite. Mom's hand reached out to ask for a sip, and Minn gave her the glass, returning to the kitchen to pour a herself a new one.

"Looks like egg salad on pumpernickel for lunch,"

she said, walking back. "And pickles. And watermelon."

"The usual."

"Plus a new pepper mill."

"Ma got a pepper mill?"

"Isn't that funny? A nice one too."

Uncle Stan took a sip from Minn's glass and went over to help prep the meal. The remaining adults continued their discussion of Grandma and her purchasing habits, and how many minutes were best for hard-boiling.

"Can I?" I pointed to my aunt's water. She handed me the glass for a sip, then took it back for herself.

"Twelve minutes," Uncle Stan called from the kitchen. "I swear by twelve on the dot!"

"Aunt Minn?"

"That is," he continued, breaking open an ice tray, "if you like your yolk just a **touch** golden . . ."

Minn glanced down at me. "Francie?"

"You gave Mom your water glass."

"Did I?"

"Yes."

"I have another!" she said, raising hers.

"But why?"

"Why what?"

"Why give Mom her own?"

Her eyebrows folded in. "Do you want a water?"

"No."

Minn touched my shoulder, confused. Mom stood near us, in between conversations, half listening to Uncle Stan's chat with Grandpa in the kitchen about his favorite basketball stars as they stirred tinkling ice into the pitcher.

"She's not catching," I said.

Over on the shelf, the big band radio announcer introduced a new song, and the speaker erupted with an assembly of trumpets. "Oh," Minn said, "of course. It's not that."

"Not what?" asked my mother, tuning in.

Minn opened up her position to include my mother, reaching out an arm to pull her close. She made some humming sounds of appreciation since they hadn't seen each other in a little while, touching the iridescent tips of my mother's shell earrings, both of them swaying above me, Minn stick-like, the swell of her belly precise through her gray tunic, my mother with her auburn hair full and gleaming, in her voluminous sea-colored skirt, steadier than usual, but still edgy, aware.

"Aunt Minn," I said again.

In the other room, someone ran the faucet, and Grandpa laughed about the demise of a certain team.

"Francie?"

I tried to keep my voice soft. "Then take a sip of her drink."

My aunt turned her head, just barely, as if to hear me better.

"Excuse me?" she said.

"Lunch!" called Grandma from the kitchen.

"Prove it," I whispered.

"Family lunchtime!" sang Grandpa, heading to the table.

Uncle Stan began walking to the table, holding the pitcher of iced tea, and Aunt Minn straightened up, away from me. All of a sudden, everything about her looked tired. I wondered, for a second, if I'd hit her by accident. She stretched out a hand slowly, as if to reach for my mother's glass, but my mother had already left by then, heading to the table with her own water glass, sitting down in what she said was her usual chair. "Come along, Francie!" she called. "Daughter of mine. Come along, come sit next to your cuckoo lady mama."

From the kitchen counter, Grandma and Uncle Stan were now bringing out the large tray of triangle sandwiches, the plates of black olives and pickles, and the bowl of small dark pink gibbous moon spheres made by the scooper Grandma had bought thirty years ago and had used to excavate hundreds of melons. Minn, who now seemed a little dazed, moved to the table enclosed by her yellow wool and firm brown buttons. "Delicious!" said Uncle Stan to the air, settling the melon bowl at his elbow. Mom blew her nose into a napkin. "I have a sore throat," she said, out of nowhere, pushing her water glass out of Minn's reach. "Keep that baby well!" she said. I had no idea if she had heard any of our earlier conversation. I was watching from the living room area, but I hadn't joined them yet, was still hovering in the space now cleared of the people, the wood-paneled walls plastered with those photographs, the piles of shiny gifts on the floor. Something felt unfinished; something else, it seemed to me, needed to happen, so at the brick ledge, on an impulse, I grabbed the tall poison bottle in its bright red cellophane wrapper. It was heavy, and tall, and felt good in my hands, so I brought it to the family table, where I pushed aside the plate of pickles and placed it neatly in the center of the lace tablecloth.

"Ah, of course!" said Grandma. "The centerpiece!" She reached behind her to a shelf and presented a small ivory-colored ceramic vase filled with pink buds. "I picked these this morning—"

"This," I said, my hand on the bottle.

"Oh, Francie, honey," said Mom, touching my arm. "That's not really a good choice for a centerpiece."

"It's the centerpiece," I said.

"Francie," said Grandma.

"I can't see anyone," said Grandpa, behind the flare of transparent red.

"Grandpa," I said, "will you please pass the olives?"

"Francie," said my mother.

The table grew quiet. Grandma pushed her little vase of flowers forward. They were the buds of camelias, like wrapped pink fists. The poison bottle, in its dress of red cellophane, dwarfed it entirely.

"We can't have a bottle of poison as a centerpiece,"

Grandma said, firmly. She raised herself taller and made a sure gesture for me to lift up the bottle and remove it. Everyone else waited. Grandma was without rival the family's authority figure, and she had been nothing but genial the whole visit so far, sitting with me in the guest room with a carved wooden box, showing me her costume jewelry and letting me wear a pair of green beaded clip-ons, even swaying to the big band songs, but now her face shut down. My mother's body shrank in her seat, and even Grandpa made himself smaller, readying for the yell, but nothing about my grandmother bothered me. Her arrows had no home inside me. I was, instead, admiring how the sunlight streaming through the red cellophane turned parts of the tablecloth into stained glass.

"Why not?" I said. "If it's a holiday gift?"

"Francie!" my grandmother boomed.

Aunt Minn began to rise in her spot, readying to intervene, to perform her usual smoothing, but I kept my hand resting on the poison bottle as lightly as if on the shoulder of a friend, and turned my face toward my grandmother's. For whatever reason, something about it all seemed to slow everyone down, and I do remember clearly how the air around us seemed to lengthen and stretch, then, the various people I was related to stopping to watch, and listen. Which was fine with me. Which was better. Grandma's face was reddening, and I could see the severity set in on her mouth, the her that had once, after a particularly difficult night, lost her temper and told my mother that if she didn't start behaving better she might take her to the daughter store and exchange her for another model, a story that had made my mother hysterical with fear, that she told me sometimes at bedtime assuring me that there was absolutely no such store but if there ever was she would always buy me at the daughter store, always the same me, no matter the price, never to worry, and there, in her dining room, the aroma of apple pie releasing into the kitchen, the place from which we would drive home that evening to avoid having to spend the night, I felt what I can only call a great mildness overtake me. As I would do with my uncle months later, to ensure I would not set foot upon an airplane, I fixed my eyes right on my grandmother's face as a simple expression of will. I could hold that kind of gaze without blinking for long periods of time. It was not an angry gaze, not at all. It held the placidity that comes from total assurance of winning.

My aunt told me later that she felt a chill at that moment, a physical cooling in the room even tucked inside her yellow woolen cardigan, and she had grabbed my mother's hand and kissed its back several times, as if there was some goodbye about to happen, some essential parting of ways. Uncle Stan sipped his water and fell into a coughing fit, and ice clinked in the pitcher of tea. Later, on the drive home, my mother had said that what I was describing to her as mildness was only the slimmest cover over which was a vast and roiling unknown. "We weren't sure what you would do," she said, shaking her head. "It was scary." I looked out the car window at the rows of pine forests in shadowy formation, their dark forms. "I just wanted the centerpiece," I said. "Would you have opened the bottle?" she asked. "The poison bottle? No. I just wanted it on the table." "Why?" "Why did I want it on the table?" "Yes." "I don't know." In the dining room, Grandma had held my stare for a minute or so, her own eyes defiant, nostrils flared, but then she shook her head with a dismissive grunt and took her seat at the head of the table. She grabbed two triangle sandwiches and poured herself tea from the pitcher and for a few minutes spoke, in muttery clipped tones, only to Grandpa. Uncle Stan began passing the primary tray around, and as everyone began to eat and talk, the meal resumed its usual tone; Grandpa interrogated Mom about her job options, and all returned to their roles.

After the pie, I carried the poison bottle around with me for the rest of the day. Aunt Minn and Uncle Stan did all the dishes, and Mom and I strolled the backyard and toured those plants she had loved, and we presented gifts to Grandma, which she accepted with curt nods, and even a half-apology for yelling at the table; "You're a tough one, Francie," she said, barking out a laugh. I gave her a nod back. The adults kept sharp eyes on me, but no one seemed concerned that I might drink from the poison myself—more that I might empty it onto the flower beds, or slip a drop into somebody's teacup. Only when we piled back in our car, and Uncle Stan and Aunt Minn had waved goodbye, heading south to spend a few days in San Francisco visiting the buffalo in Golden Gate Park and eating mounds of sourdough as happy, dutiful tourists, only then did I hand the bottle back through the open car window after asking my grandmother to promise that she wouldn't send it to the doctor anymore. She didn't answer me, but stood on the lawn with the bottle in her hand like she was holding a crackling fire. "She's not a mistake," I said out the window. "Drive safely," Grandma said, "thank you for coming." "He did not ruin her," I said. "Sorry, Ma," said my mother, leaning over me to wave out the passenger side, "happy birthday." She put the car into drive, fir trees springing up in pointy clusters at the sides of the road, as we turned the corner to head to the 5 North.

35

"But he did," she said quietly, smoking out the driver's-side window, an hour or so later, when she thought I was asleep.

36

When Esther finally brought my blanket back to elementary school, after I'd called and asked her for it under my mother's watch that morning, "Please bring it to school, it has little sheep on it, thank you," it was after I'd already left town. She brought it on the Monday after the hammer smash, and by then I was deep in my window seat on the train, halfway down the western edge of the country, looking out at the Shakespeare billboards fronting even more clusters of trees advertising the upcoming summer theater bill in Ashland, Oregon: **Hamlet. Twelfth Night. Death of a Salesman**. I retained no love for the blanket, but it showed up in Burbank a few weeks later anyway, in a yellow puffy package on the counter mailed from Portland with my name on it and the neatly folded graying cloth inside. A colorful card from one of the volunteer mothers said, **We're thinking of you, Francie. Here's someone who might help a little bit**. Aunt Minn was in the other room trying to tend to a fussy Vicky in the rocking chair with her breast, and I stood there at the counter with the sound of a car radio blaring commercials from outside picking at that word. **Someone**. Obviously, it was a well-meaning volunteer mother who had searched my cubby and figured the blanket was important and had taken the time to find my address and fold it so carefully, but as I dumped the fabric out of the envelope, the world split into the two parts it had become so many times before: into those who could adorably call a blanket a someone, and those of us who, just weeks earlier, had listened to her mother racked with sobs over the decimated bodies of cotton-stuffed lions. Who, just months before, had watched her aunt drink a new glass of water just in case there was any invented chance of passing the illness along to her fetus via spit. I slid the card into the paper shredder.

Even the sight of the blanket bothered me, but I didn't know how to dispose of it; I walked around the house, but any trash can felt conspicuous, scissors wouldn't cut it well, burning would be too messy. More than anything, I wanted to slip it into the invisible. Vicky had started to cry again; she had exited the womb a healthy baby with an intact head, a baby with everything just where it was supposed to be, who had passed all her tests, and was growing in all the ways hoped, but who still had a lot of trouble burping, and while Aunt Minn patted her back over and over in the baby room, singing clips of songs, saying sshh, sshh, please baby, please, with a catch in her voice, some kind of lullaby rotation cube spinning light patterns on the floor, I went to the doorway of the nursery and told my aunt I had just received an old baby blanket in the mail; would it please be okay if I gave it to the baby? Aunt Minn, her face hazy with exhaustion, living right at the rim of overwhelm, said that was very generous of me, absolutely, please, and we both twitched a little in amazement when the moment I draped the blanket on my aunt's shoulder, the baby burped, rested her head right on it, and within seconds had fallen asleep.

Years later, when I came home from the visit to the neurologist holding on to the dead roses that had emerged from the damask curtains at Deena's house, something similar occurred. Vicky was older then, but everything of mine still had a pull on her, and as soon as we drove up, she ran out of the house in her bare feet and followed me to the side yard, bombarding me with questions: how was it? did the doctor say anything new? are you all right? and I told her the doctor had been fine, nothing new, all was okay, nothing to worry about, but she stood by my shoulder and raised up on her toes to look in as I laid the roses in the green garbage can in the side yard among grass cuttings and crackling strands of dead bougainvillea as gathered by the gardener on Tuesdays. I had told her earlier where the roses had come from. I had told her I did not plan to keep them. So, it was not a huge surprise when later, after I let the lid of the bin drop without ceremony, out my window, when night had fallen on the garden and she thought I was doing homework, I saw as Vicky sneaked through the side door, tiptoed to the bins, and carefully lifted one of the roses from the pile. "Vick, that you out there?" called Aunt Minn from the living room, where she was flipping through channels. "Just checking something for homework!" Vicky called back, side door locking. By then, I had locked myself in my room for the night, which I still did despite the fact that her skull had knit together years earlier without interference, which I still did even though Deena had invited me out with her and another friend that night, to the movie-plex, to see a thriller; no, I preferred the sanctity and simplicity of this enclosed chamber, and I could hear the faint sounds of Vicky entering the living room, the two of them laughing at a show, Uncle Stan making a bowl of popcorn, Vicky likely tucked into the bone of her mother's shoulder, cozy, the rose somewhere nearby, on a shelf, maybe, or a table. When I asked her about it the next day, both of us home from school, the trash trucks come and gone, her sitting cross-legged on her maroon quilt doing math drills, she knelt down and opened the drawer on her nightstand with the brass key she wore around her neck, and there it was, nestled on a scrap of fabric, petals dry and cracking. All her most precious things were in there: the azure marble she'd found once in Aunt Minn's coat pocket, a skillful drawing of a Siamese cat by her friend Lola, a whittled spoon from Grandpa. "Why do you want it?" I asked. Outside, the tall sycamore pressed its leaves against her window. "I just want it." "It won't become anything else." "That's fine." She glared at me with force in her eyes, but as we sat there the force began falling in on itself, turning inside out until it became, in an instant, begging. "Please don't take it away," she said, starting to cry. "It's so special to me." She held it to her cheek, and then lowered it back to the drawer to settle on its remnant of dun-colored satin. "The only flower in the world that didn't come from a seed," she said. "Except the other two." "Stop, Francie! Don't you see? I'll have this when I'm an old lady. I will pass it along to my children. If there was a fire, I would get it first—" "First?" "Of the **things,** please. You gave it up, Francie. It belongs to me now."

37

It all mattered to Vicky. Vicky's personal essay about me. Vicky's monologue for her theater class playwriting unit about my mother's excessive blanket delivery on the Fourth of July. Vicky's drawer of memorabilia. Vicky's idea of stickiness that turned into the memory tent.

On that first day of the tent's use, after she'd come over and built it with me, she called as soon as she got home from school. "Tell me, tell me!" she said, "how was it?" and I could hear her moving things around in the kitchen, undoing the dishwasher, stacking bowls. "Fine," I said, slowly. "Kind of random. All I remembered today was how the babysitter had this fringy scarf on her television." "Cool." "And her cat." "You mean Hattie?" I laughed. "I should just interview you," I said. She jangled some silverware. "I told Mom about what we made, and she thought it was really interesting, but she's a tiny bit worried about it. I mean, I think it's amazing, but she thinks you might be isolating yourself." I moved over to the balcony glass window to look out at the new protruding orange tent shape. It had only been a day by that point, but I thought I could already feel it gaining something inside, vapor steeping, waiting for me. "Will you tell her it's a way to un-isolate myself?" I said, stepping forward, pressing my nose to the glass of the balcony door; "It's like the freeze tag." "Where you were more connected to the kids at school while you were frozen than when you were talking to them at a table?" "Exactly." "That still seems really crazy to me." "But it is true." Vicky paused. I could hear her gently dropping spoons into a drawer. Like it had been with the freeze tag, if I concentrated and listened, I could feel now, for a second, the presence of the world buzzing outside me, the cars on the street, the people stepping into the stores, the children on the playgrounds, my existence inside it. How I might, over time, form some kind of outline in this way. "Aren't you lonely, Francie?" Vicky asked. "Sure," I said. "I mean, sitting there in a tent all day and mailing packages?" "It won't be all day." "Do you feel distant from me now? Like are you secretly playing freeze tag in your mind or something?" She waited. Plates clinked into piles. "You have your own mother, you know," I said, breathing a smudge onto the glass. "With her own stuff," I said. Vicky laughed. "You think?" I breathed out until the smudge was as large as my face. "Make your own tent," I said.

38

By their adolescences, Elaine and Minnie looked so different that strangers in lines at the grocery store or doctors' offices laughed out loud when they found out they were siblings. At that point, it was like the sisters had been born in different dimensions, like Grandma Bea had, during labor, wandered out of her hospital room into a space-time warp where she delivered two children from varying proportional systems, who would look almost identical for the first few years of life, until one shrank and the other expanded, not in terms of weight, but of something more elemental. Aunt Minn appears more sleek and efficient than my mother: smaller eyes, bones, gestures, words, more porcelain in style, and delicacy of movement. My mother, woman of enthusiasms, has that roiling bountiful hair, generous features and gestures, and when well an appreciation of jazz piano and vibrators, full moons, gold-plated oyster forks. The man she is currently dating, Edward, the pianist, says when they make a plan to go out, "the lights of the city brighten." His own eyes glow as he grabs her hand, as we leave her room at Hawthorne House to walk over together to the living room area, where she will soon be singing as part of the post-lunch show. I'm here for my annual fall visit, a few months into the memory tent, the visit timed to coincide with this performance of selections from **Pal Joey** as accompanied by Edward and his friend the percussionist, and we stroll the main hall together and step into the living room, and when we do, to my complete shock, the whole area, my usual favorite part of the visit, the place in which I have spent so many updating afternoons, reveals itself to be entirely redecorated. Chrome-armed sofas and new plastic coffee tables. Solid-color rugs. Enlarged photographs of birds and flowers. Particleboard desks. Wicker trash cans. My mother sees my face, tells me someone discovered a month or so ago that those beautiful raw silk lime green parlor chairs in which we sat, side by side, over so many years, had all been absolutely seething with termites. "You wouldn't believe how fast they fixed it!" she says, laughing. "It took two days? Was it two, Edward?" "It seemed like a minute," he says, smiling into her eyes. They head to their spots, her greeting everyone like the star of a show, which she is, him settling at the piano, which is the same, and before I take my seat, and the show begins, I stop and ask a staff member in the hall if she happens to know where the seascapes that used to hang on the walls in those golden frames went: the ones with the crashing waves? The wild storm-clouded skies? The pail? Maybe there's one in a closet somewhere I could take home? I'd found, I tell her, so much solace in them over the years. My voice surprises me, shaking with urgency, and the tall woman in scrubs hears it, nods at me—we've had many short conversations over the years—and pulls me aside, away from the remaining trickle of residents heading in to get their seats. In the corner, she tells me in a hushed, almost conspiratorial voice that she's very sorry, and she loved those pictures too, but by the time they dragged the furniture and paintings outside to get picked up by sanitation services, everything was literally disintegrating in their hands. "It was actually kind of incredible," she says, widening her eyes. "Watching them dissolve. It was almost like they had never existed in the first place." She flutters her fingers in the air. "Like they returned to dust."

My mother sings wonderfully, and gets a standing ovation from the residents, and Edward hugs her in a way that seems kind, and she introduces me to everyone as her greatest accomplishment, but I think only about the disintegrating paintings during the flight home. They are significant to me in a way I can't quite pinpoint. It's evening by then, and the sun is setting, and the dust motes floating in the body of the plane are lit into a goldenness. Outside the windows, the landscape moves below us, farmlands again, mountain peaks, my own thinking, and by the time the wheels bump to landing, I think it might be because it means that any speck of dust in the world may have once been part of a beautiful painting. My mother looked happy in her bronze eye shadow, happier than I've ever seen her. My baggage is the last to arrive on the baggage claim.

39

The babysitter was finishing in the bathroom, running the faucet, humming a song. I had only a minute. I could not leave the butterfly in the water glass in her apartment, but I did not have a book handy in which to press it, or a baggie, or anything to preserve it in a proper way, so I picked up the glass, and when I swallowed it down, the wings scratched like a finely leafed lettuce down my throat, with only the faintest prickings from legs and antennae.

The faucet turned off, and the babysitter opened the door to return to the living room. She had clipped a festive pink rhinestone barrette into her hair for wherever she would go after dropping me off.

"Thirsty girl!" she said, smiling at the empty glass. "Ready?"

"Ready."

PART FOUR

Beetle

40

On a Saturday afternoon later in the fall, Vicky asks if she can come over to my apartment to work on the final final draft of her essay. We're at the end of October now, and she tells me, sprawled on the carpet, that Aunt Minn has been checking on her weekend plans again in this pretend-casual way that Vicky hates, and she really appreciates how empty my apartment is, how quiet, with the balcony door open and an occasional breeze floating in even though it's been such a hot fall, so bright in the direct sunlight that I can feel burn rising to the surface of my skin in minutes. She says she likes how I have such little furniture, even though she also thinks it's creepy. "Both," she says, stretching out her legs, "definitely both."

We are leaning against one of the walls, as usual, looking at some of her final sentence changes, while also sorting through a surplus I found over the weekend from a woman moving to a much smaller apartment in Chicago due to a hopeful new romance.

The Butterfly Lampshade

The woman had taken me on a tour of her ceramic and blown glass vases, set on card tables of varying heights, vases she'd collected for thirty years, plus some great wooden bracelets, and a scarf I set aside for my mother of the vibrant reds and purples she loves the most. I circle a line in Vicky's essay about the lock. "This could still be sharper," I say. "I mean, to say it was an honor is a little much." She's flat on the floor now, leaning on a pillow, and tries to scribble on the draft in the air with a red pen, but the ink just bends on the folded paper. "But it was an honor," she says after a minute, reaching her eyes to mine. "I want to say honor." "It's just a little over-the-top, don't you think?" "Not if it's true, Francie." There's a knock at the door. We look at each other. "Did you order anything?" she asks, hopeful. In the peephole is the warped and intent face of that building manager, who lives those few doors down. She has never knocked on my door before. "Can I speak with you for a moment?" she asks when I open up.

41

The train to Los Angeles was set to leave at two p.m., but the babysitter told me it was good to get there early so we could meet the steward and make sure everything was settled for the trip. Together, we gathered my bags, and I glanced around the loft until we headed downstairs to the #9 covered bus stop at the end of the block. Outside, the day was beautiful, a vibrant demonstration of spring, the city sparkling with a green and varied aliveness, and on the bus, commuters sat in chairs, reading, looking out windows, two friends talking with excitement about a party they'd attended the night before. The babysitter and I were both quiet; she was thinking of other things, or trying to be respectful of my transition, and I was in a daze about my body and what was in it. The new queasiness and hint of elation I felt while holding on to the greasy silver pole of the bus and watching the squat brown buildings and stores pass by.

"Francie," the babysitter said, before we arrived

at our stop. She swiveled to face me. Her eyes were serious. "I've been thinking. I would like to send you a package in your new home. Would that be okay with you?"

"What kind of package?"

She let out a breath and smiled. "Well, I don't know if a surprise would be better, but you know how you were asking about the lamp? The butterfly lamp? I was thinking a lot about it, and I would like very much to give it to you. It would make me happy to give it to you as a gift for your new home."

"You mean the one in the living room?"

"Yes. The one we were talking about."

The bus passed my mother's and my favorite burger joint, where my mother had called the french fries ringlets.

"Thank you very much, Shrina," I said. "But I don't want it anymore."

"You don't?"

"No," I said. "It should stay with you."

"Are you sure? You were so interested the other day, and I know I said that I wanted to keep it but—"

"I don't want it anymore."

We descended the steps of the bus and walked into the train station, stands and stalls surrounding emitting a brew of donut fry oil and magazine cover ink. The building was warm with light, and filled with people, out and about, ready to travel, and the babysitter collected my prepaid ticket at Will Call and reached for my hand, explaining how we were going to the café now to meet the steward. "Well, if you ever change your mind," she said, squeezing.

"Can I hold my ticket?"

She handed it over, searching the station for the café.

"Shrina?"

She turned to me. "Yes?" She kept her eyes scanning as we walked, likely trying to figure out which person at the various tables was the steward—the old bearded man with the newspaper? One of the two suited men sitting and talking over a scone?

I said it in a whisper first. The babysitter turned. She hadn't heard the words, but something in my tone had registered, had bothered her. "What was that, Francie?"

"There's a bug in me," I said, louder. I felt a wave of pure giddiness when I said it.

She had been so consistent the whole weekend: kind, steady, pretty, upbeat, but as soon as I spoke, she tugged me over to the side by a cement pole, away from the traffic of walkers. "Hey!" she said, kneeling in front of me. Her forehead tightened. "Your mother wasn't well when she said that, Francie. Okay? You are beautiful inside and out. Do you understand?"

Her eyes locked on mine, searching.

"Francie? There is nothing, **nothing** wrong with you."

I blinked back at her, at those lucent obsidian eyes.

"Francie?"

"Yes, Shrina."

"Can you tell me if you understand?"

"Yes."

"Please, Francie. What is it that you understand?"

"That I am beautiful inside and out. You know about the bug?"

"Your uncle mentioned it."

"When?"

"When? While you were in the car, I think. He was concerned. I am too. We all care about you very much."

I watched the light catching on the sparkling pink rhinestones of her barrette. Commuters and travelers rushing to and fro behind her. I could still taste the tiny slags of butterfly feet as they'd dragged over my tongue.

"Why?" I asked, after a moment.

"Why what?"

"Why do you care about me so much?"

Her eyebrows pinched in. "It's hard to explain," she said. "There's this line between us. We are connected, so we have a line of care between us."

"But we don't," I told her, holding her gaze. "I will get on the train, and I will never see you again."

"Oh, we will see each other again!" she said. "I'm sure of it."

I looked at her closely. "Shrina," I said.

42

The building manager stands in the doorframe with her usual gray ponytail and floral T-shirt. She told me once that she has lived and worked here in this building for over ten years, after moving to Los Angeles years ago from Kansas to try to get a break in the movies. She makes the other part of her living doing pet portraiture.

"I thought you'd have more stuff by now," she says once the door is open, scanning the living room and its population of brown boxes.

"Hi again," she says to Vicky, who is still sitting on the floor.

"Hi."

The building manager says she is sorry to interrupt, but it's not about the balcony today; she heard something else, and she wanted to check it out with me, just find out a little bit more information if I wouldn't mind. "It's about Jose," she says, raising her eyebrows brightly. I glance behind me at Vicky, who is now busily at work on a large box, wrapping the tissue paper carefully around the tall rose-swirled vase, adding the flower sticker to bind it. "Can we talk in the hall?" I ask. Vicky looks up. The building manager takes one step back. She picks at the hair at the fray of her ponytail. She's still entirely in the apartment, and her voice is not low. "I was talking to him this morning," she says, "and I just wanted to make sure your arrangement was all aboveboard and legal. I just don't want any funny business in my building," she says. "No funny business," I say, "no funny business at all." Behind us, Vicky crumples a tissue paper overly loudly. "He says he uses a front door key to get in?" the manager asks. Yes, I say. "And he says your bedroom is locked why? Something about sleepwalking?" I tell her that it's just as a safety measure. That he's up early for his work at the racetrack anyway. That right before he goes to work, he just stops by really fast to unlock. It's probably four-thirty in the morning. No one else is up. We've had this setup for years, and no one has ever complained, and his wife also does it on Mondays so he can sleep in. "And you pay them?" the manager asks. I tell her we even signed a paper together in case anyone ever had any questions. I can show you, I tell her, if you want. Her eyes watch me intently, little bright drills, and behind us now is total silence. I can hear Vicky listening, can hear the shape and quality of her listening, which moves into all the space behind us, and when I turn it's easy to track her eyes as they drift over to my bedroom door, to the lock there, which under scrutiny is clearly facing the wrong direction.

The building manager peers past me again, into the living room. "You really don't like furniture, do you? Is that another sleepwalking thing?"

"Just keeping things simple."

"That's one word for it." She laughs. "Okay. That sounds okay. Just keep it all on the up-and-up." She waves at Vicky, who is sitting surrounded by all the boxes, and barely raises a hand to wave back. The building manager closes the door. We can hear the soft padding of her footsteps down the hall and the click of her own door as it opens, and shuts.

43

When I turn back to the living room fully, Vicky's eyes are still on the door, and she's quiet. She's stopped wrapping things, and her hands rest in her lap. She has had no idea that the practice that inspired her personal statement continued through my time at UCLA with my dorm roommate and suitemates whom I bribed with cafeteria desserts, to my previous apartment on Riverton near the airport with a different neighbor, into now. She pulls over a plastic sheet, pops a few packing bubbles with her thumb. Downstairs, on the street, someone leans long and hard on their car horn, and when the noise stops, she looks at me directly and asks, in a low voice, if it has been going on the whole time. **This** is how I know Jose? She'd figured the locking ended when I moved out. She is, she says, surprised. I move about the living room, making stacks, tidying up the tissue paper pile, neatening up my packing areas. The traffic flow down on the street settles into whooshes of sound, and her stillness is frightening to me, the lack of understanding in her face, and after all the wrapping excess has been placed into its elected spots, when order has been arbitrarily imposed upon the space, I go and sit down beside her.

In a halting voice, speaking my words to the floor, pulling at the carpet fibers, I explain that it has been going on the whole time, yes, and that I've never told her this before, and it may come as a shock, but that in truth, the truth is, she was the source. How it was her fontanelle that made me ask Aunt Minn for the lock in the first place, how I was so new to the house then and checking every single room for sharp tools because I was constantly imagining plunging them inside her head and destroying her brain. Kind of like the doctor did by bumping my mother against the table, I tell her, shaking my head. I suppose I wanted to do that same damage to you. I start to apologize, but by then, she is up, standing at my bedroom door, turning the knob back and forth, clicking the lock in and out, just like she used to do at home when we were standing in the hall together before bed, talking about anything, making dumb jokes about farts and monkeys, and then, out of nowhere, she bursts out laughing. "What," I say, and she knocks on her skull. "Feel it," she says, pressing down on her hair. "Come on, feel it! It's **fine**." She says it is all ridiculous to her because I never did anything bad like that, nothing even close, and that it is just the most obvious thing in the world to everyone else that I love her. She reaches to the floor and throws a stray sock ball at me; "God!" she says. I stand up, swaying a little. I tell her that's true, that I do love her, but she shouldn't take it so lightly because one never knows what one is capable of. Hadn't anyone told her the story of the poison bottle? She tilts her head. "You mean the one where you took on Grandma like a badass?" I pick up the sock ball and place it carefully on a shelf. "Or when I sent Mom over the back of the chair?" "That was not you." "It was partly me," I say, "plus, there are always babies," finally meeting her eyes. She stares at me. "What, you think you're going to wake up in the middle of the night, break into someone's house, and find a baby to hurt?" She spits out another laugh. I focus on the sock ball, rerolling it together. People get consumed by drives they don't understand all the time, I tell her, quietly. There are real people who go crazy all of a sudden, like bing. Couldn't that be me? Why wouldn't that be me?

She leans her head on the doorframe. She has a greenish bruise on her inner arm from the tech rehearsal for **Our Town**. She showed me earlier. The metal gel frame grazed her elbow.

"You know what, Francie?" she says, and her eyes soften. "Let's do this. I'll come over for a sleepover. Okay? You tell Jose he has the morning off on Sunday. I have another tech in the morning but I'll come over after and I will sleep in the living room on that horrible couch of yours and you leave your bedroom door open. We can even take the lock off. I'll bring my pepper spray from my self-defense class, and if you turn into a zombie monster murderer, I'll spray you down. Okay? Will you do that? Saturday afternoon. We can have dinner together too. You pay for dinner since you already feel so bad about everything. I loved that pizza last time. Get the same kind. Enough already."

And she sweeps out of the room as if to make an exit even though there's nowhere else to go.

44

Our grandfather did sleepwalk, but he hurt himself only once. Usually, according to Grandma, he started awake and then fell back into bed, but once he did leave their bedroom and opened up the backyard door to step out onto the porch. This was the same rickety porch I would stand on with my mother years later at Grandma's birthday event, with the gnarled wisteria branches torquing through the wooden white trellis diamonds. My mother says she remembers it well; she was out on the mattress, having recently started sleeping most nights outside, under sheets that each morning had to be hung to dry on a line after a light wetting from the dew. She stirred awake and there was a silhouette, backlit by the yellow living room light that stayed on in case she needed to use the bathroom. She flinched, frightened. "Dad?" she asked, in a wavery voice, and the figure mumbled something about how he needed to fill the car up for the drive. Moonlight shone pale beams on the grasses. "Dad," she said, "it's the middle of the night," and he said that the car was low on gas and they needed it full for the trip. "What trip?" "To the zoo," he said. They had not been to the zoo in many years. She had loved the zoo; it had been one of her favorite places. He started to walk off the porch toward the side bushes and tripped on the step and fell and twisted his ankle, and my mother called for my grandmother, and the two led him back inside, my mother nude, my grandmother in some kind of patchwork cotton nightgown. In the kitchen, my grandmother attended to the scrape on his knee and bandaged his ankle. Pain had returned him to the land of the awake, and he scratched his head and apologized and told my mother to cover herself and after a few minutes, leaned on my grandmother, who guided him back to bed. Minnie slept through it all. My mother and her body, further dispatches from **Le Déjeuner sur l'herbe,** returned to the yard and slipped back under the sheets. In the morning, my grandfather remembered only parts of it, and he wore the bandage for a few weeks, sustaining a sprain. My mother told me she had been frightened by the surprise, but not of him, his taciturn self, his often annoyed and distant self, and always wondered instead if it had been his way of checking on her. She felt it acknowledged her mattress location as a kind of room. "He did not pick the front yard," she said when she told me, nodding her head as if to seal in the idea. "Where the car was actually parked." It is the main moment she retells when she says she felt a kind of love from her father.

45

Friday, I sit in the tent for an hour with nothing. My mind is edgy. The canvas is hot. The only memories I can summon up—birthdays, trips to Disneyland—look suspiciously like the photos I've seen multiple times in Aunt Minn's carefully constructed scrapbooks. I consider canceling the weekend plan with Vicky to clear my head, claiming illness, or yard sale conflicts, but whatever reason I give she will surely smoke out; when I was in high school, she caught me in every lie I told about why I was past curfew or who I might be meeting, even if it was all motivated by Deena and her dubious online dating plans. Plus, she's stubborn. One time, she got all her middle school classmates to write notes to Aunt Minn and Uncle Stan so she could go on the field trip to Descanso Gardens instead of her previously scheduled visit to the dentist. A few of the notes are still on the fridge, so many years later, yellowed by time: "Let V. join the botanists!" "Floral, not fluoride!" Burbank is actually named for a dentist, so it was, in its way, a layered rebellion. She went on the trip, of course; the dental appointment was not at all pressing. Later, Aunt Minn confessed to me during another one of our late-night dimmed living room glass-of-wine confession talks that she'd heard that some people received actual radio transmissions through their metallic fillings and she had wanted to go to the dentist that day to replace those in her daughter because, she told me, looking away, if Vicky ever did happen to hear voices, she wanted to be very, very clear where they were coming from.

She and I sat together in the living room that night, in silence. Vicky went to Descanso and frolicked around the orange fences of the Japanese garden, and at a later date, had her fillings switched to composite. As did I.

46

On Saturday, I do my grocery shopping and then wrap packages by myself for a few hours. It was a fruitful week at the yard sales. There is a pale pink fluted-glass bowl a woman gave away for a quarter off Wilton in Hollywood because it had been tainted by the disappointment of a broken friendship, and I wash it and take all the ache away with my sponge and present it blemish-free for forty bucks to Donna in Milwaukee who gives me five stars and says my packaging is excellent. I dry-clean and fold a designer scarf and bracelet trio that belonged to a dead woman sold by her lead-eyed daughter in Woodland Hills that has changed into new silken and gold accentuators of vitality for savvy purchaser Marine in El Cajon. An old friend from college reaches out and asks if I want to meet up for dinner and I tell her I'm busy with a difficult work project but I'd love to at a later point and ask a few things about herself and that is that.

Vicky knocks at around four p.m., wearing some

kind of red wraparound sweater that looks like a blanket that reminds me intensely of my mother's fashion impulses. She has a small backpack on her shoulder. She helps me pack again for a little while, stuffing more bubble wrap as needed, taping the tissue paper, adding the little flower sticker again for flair. We order another pizza, as requested, and open the box on the floor, and she eats it with her legs spread wide like a dancer, sprinkling red pepper flakes I have never seen her use before, telling me about the ridiculousness of Wendell who plays Doc Gibbs and how he seems to think it's okay to do every line the exact same way every time they run the show. "I mean, listening, right? Where is the listening?" She explains how she decided on pale blue downstage that upstage shifts to a darker burgundy. "It's really eerie and good. They still kind of vanish into the back, but in a warmish way." I bring her the cookies I bought earlier, her favorite, mint chocolate and cello-shaped, fanned out on a small plate, and for a fleeting second imagine myself as the babysitter, the ultimate host.

When she's done, she clears her plate and goes to peek at the tent on the balcony. It looks far more ragged now, several months exposed to the elements, bleached on one side to a pale yellow from the sun. She pulls the sliding door lock lever up.

"You realize you can't go in anymore, right?" I say.

She turns around, surprised. "Really?"

"I don't even go in unless I'm staying for a little while. There's stuff in there now."

"I can stay for a little while."

"It's only for me, Vicky. Sorry."

She clicks the lock back down, tapping at the glass door with her fingernails.

"Real stuff?"

"It's hard to explain. Nothing solid, no."

Her nails make small, irritable sounds.

"Everything's so locked up in here!" she says, flouncing onto the couch.

We watch a movie on my computer, a romantic comedy about a bookstore. She asks midway, the movie paused so she can use the bathroom, if I told Jose to take the morning off. I tell her yes, and how he was surprised, how he nodded his head in what could only be called approval. "Of course he did!" she says, emerging, going to the kitchen to pour herself a glass of water. "No one but you thinks you're a psycho."

We are both a little nervous at bedtime, even though I brushed my teeth in the same bathroom as her for at least eleven years. I know how she brushes and spits and rinses. She is, at this point, more familiar to me than my mother. She closes the bathroom door while I'm cleaning up the pizza debris in the kitchen and changes into her pajamas which have the happy/sad faces of drama on them in yellow and black given to her by an overly literal-minded aunt on Uncle Stan's side. "They're so overdone they're wonderful," she says, grinning. "Right? I'm going to wear them on the first night in the dorm and see who runs away screaming and that might be exactly who I pursue as a friend."

I ask her if the applications are in, and she says as of yesterday. All set, all sent. She brushes off her hands. "And what a perfect way to finish the essay."

"You mean sleeping over?"

She gives me a look. Unzips her backpack, and eyes my room.

"Okay," she says, "so the truth is, I don't trust you not to sneak up and lock yourself in in the middle of the night. You'll have to take the lock off."

"I'm not going to be able to sleep."

"Oh, you'll sleep a little." She rummages in the main pocket. "I also brought a screwdriver," brandishing it.

She is so good with this stuff. She has it off in seconds. The bedroom already feels so loose to me, like it will spill all its roomness into the world, me included. With the gaping hole in the door and the lock on the floor with its surgical droppings of screws and bolts everything begins to lose a little contact with sense and reason. The monster feeling of the loft returning, those woven corner darknesses beginning to fluctuate on their own. I stare at her, glassy-eyed. She runs to the couch, tucks her screwdriver under her pillow, "Good, right? Super sharp!" and also shows me the pepper spray and how they taught her to use it in her self-defense elective: aim, spray, don't hesitate. "I'm all set, Francie," she says, stretching out on the couch pillows. "You just try."

47

My grandmother wrote me one birthday card during my adolescence. It was the only birthday card I ever remember receiving from her, and in it she told me she had seen the doctor who'd injured my mother at a local harvest festival event for the community, and they had had a conversation about the poison bottle and she wanted me to know there were no hard feelings on the doctor's side. In her looping old-fashioned handwriting, she wrote how she understood that possibly what I had taken issue with on her birthday event years ago was the red cellophane holiday aspect of the delivery. Was that correct? If so, she understood. She now opted to send the doctor the poison bottle directly, in a brown paper bag, and he'd said at the event that he understood the purpose of the ritual and had taken to donating it to local exterminators. She also said she was proud of my mother and how she had raised me well for many years, against so many people's expectations and concerns, and she was pleased that my mother was playing an active role at the center (my grandmother always called Hawthorne House "the center" for unknown reasons). She, my grandmother, was not well, and did not know when or if we would see each other again, but she said it gave her relief to know that with Minnie and Stan, and later me and even Victoria, my mother would always be in capable hands if need be. She, my grandmother, was thinking more about the family as she approached the closing days of her life, and for whatever reason, she found that she often remembered that particular day of the birthday party and my choice of centerpiece.

Happy birthday, she wrote. Here is twenty dollars. Please buy yourself something nice.

When my grandmother died, my mother called and wept on the phone to Minn, and when Minn passed the phone to me, drifting off to some other part of the house to do her own mourning in private, I dug the card out to read my mother the part about the pride to which she listened silently. The twenty-dollar bill was still there in the fold, green, gray, worn. I was a little sad about my grandmother, who lived in my mind as a kind of rock formation, but something about the money bothered me, like a payoff of some sort, so I placed it in an envelope and mailed it to my mother a few weeks later, after the funeral, with a note scrawled saying I had found it on the pavement at the high school and right when I spotted it someone had shouted "Elaine!"

across the quad, so of course I had to send it to her. I knew she would believe and appreciate the story, which was entirely invented, and the twenty-dollar bill, like the future vases and scarves of my job, was now scrubbed of its history and only cash to her. A gift from her own mother, invisible to them both.

48

The first night of the locked door, so many years ago, after my aunt had gone to the hardware store per my request and bought me the lock, I initially sat close to the door's edge, talking to her. There were many fast sensations that night—the nervous feeling of door-checking, the flash of terror realizing I was stuck, the sound of my aunt's questions and Vicky hiccuping in my uncle's arms, but mostly, primarily, the room took shape around me. It was even better than it had been when I had control over the opening and closing of the lock myself on Taylor Street in Portland; in Burbank, the moment the door clicked shut, and the bolt engaged, objects became meaningful in their spots. Or they returned to meaning, they became, again, meaningful, when earlier they had been haphazard and without weight. With the limit of the door in place, the room became obviously where I was, and where I would then stay for the course of the next ten or so hours. In the mornings, before the task passed to

Vicky, my aunt could be counted on to knock and unlock at six-thirty a.m. when I was supposed to get up, and sometimes she even did it earlier if she was awake, worrying I might be hungry, or thirsty, or lonely, or sad. She found, she told me, that the sight of the knob on its horizontal setting gave her a bad feeling, "like being on a sinking ship," she said, one morning, in her shell-pink bathrobe, greeting me with anxious eyes. But my ship was well. At least in this way, I had found a kind of resource for myself. I left the window a crack open in case of fire, but I didn't have any impulse to jump, and did not worry that I would fling myself out in the middle of the night. Vicky was safe as pie in her bassinet, and during the day I could even enjoy her and play with her without fear that I would kill her as soon as the grown-ups fell asleep.

When I think back upon that transition, besides Aunt Minn's and Uncle Stan's kindness toward me, which was obviously very important, the door lock was the other crucial component that allowed me to adapt more or less successfully to my new life in California.

(This was the essay I sometimes wrote in my mind as a counterpoint to Vicky's.)

49

Vicky sleeps on the couch in her usual way, neck exposed, her mouth slightly open, one leg hitched high like a leaping gazelle. I can see her through the open doorframe of my room. In my own bed, all I can think about is the action of picking up the parts of the lock and rescrewing them back into place. Those little brass screws boring into the door, into their spots. I think about it over and over again, tossing, alert, and after some hours pass, get out of bed. Everything in the apartment feels unhinged, literally, like there are no doors left either and we may as well be sleeping on the sidewalk, and the only place that beckons to me at all is the tent. To replace one formerly effective small space with another. I tiptoe past Vicky on the couch, and she shifts and mutters as I go by. "You," she says, softly, dream-soaked. "You." Out on the balcony, I leave the glass door open in case she needs anything, unzip the tent, climb in, pull to closed. I've never been in at night before, with the night traffic creating new arrangements of sound, and a faint pleasurable strand of coldness moving through the air. Lights burn in the corner from the infusion of streetlamps, and the rest of the orange of the interior canvas is darker, almost black. I am entirely awake. I return to thinking about the day of the train ride. The train ride, with its two fleeting visitors. The train ride with the kind steward taking care of me. The train ride with its vistas of edged mountains and wavy grasses and tall conifers. I feel this rush toward all of them, the babysitter, the steward, the conductor, the woman in the suit, the man in the suit, their faces vivid, even leering. The dark intensifies them, and the memories move in, close and active, like nocturnal creatures scuttling in the shadows. With Vicky's breathing faintly audible in the living room it is all reminding me so much of being in the babysitter's apartment that first night, her own sleep-breathing up in the loft, the night when the darkness began to fold in on itself, and silent cogs stirred in an ancient machine. It is an unmistakable echo.

50

We found the steward sitting at a small table with a poppy seed bagel and square of translucent brown paper and an orange juice carton. I remember he was wearing a scarlet red jacket with a small embroidered black train on the front pocket. Both the babysitter and my uncle had told me about him: "He sounds very reliable," "He's always been a good kid," but I did laugh out loud when he waved us over; he had unusually long legs and a long neck with a large Adam's apple and even an eight-year-old could tell he was awkward. I imagined my mother meeting him as she met most new adults taking care of me, babysitters, teachers, shaking his hand by embracing it with two of her own, and thanking him over and over with her aching, skitchy eyes. He greeted me warmly, and said something about my uncle, even though second cousin or not, he was just, at that point, the next in the line of adults to me, the baton passing.

While the café radio rumbled out a song, the

babysitter took out a piece of paper and the two of them huddled together, going over whatever formal details needed to be shared. I don't remember any mention of his name. The babysitter glanced at me and then told him in a low voice that I liked oatmeal in the morning, "with brown sugar," and that every day I cried in bursts, but that sitting by me seemed to be the best way of support. "She doesn't sleep with a special stuffed animal or anything," the babysitter said, "but she does like a light on." "Any kind of light?" "I'm sure she'll tell you," the babysitter said, after we finished our snack and began walking toward the quay, "but she seems to prefer something dim."

I tripped along between the two of them. The butterfly was settling inside me, and despite the feeling that I was floating, and that the signs lining the train station could at any moment shake off their stands just like the butterfly had, as if everything—hamburger, cartoon dog, letters—might be on the verge of popping into the world, plus the insistent warm sensation despite evidence that I was bleeding out the back of my head, it was not such a bad thing to feel like an official topic of conversation, a subject to learn. Once we were boarding, I hugged the babysitter briefly, but she was already transforming into a bystander, her face mutating into foreignness, and I mounted the stairs to our train car, where the steward placed my black rolly suitcase on a high shelf, asking if I'd prefer him to sit next to me, or across. "Across," I murmured, and he nodded with a professional briskness. In minutes, I had a row to myself, with a window to myself, and he settled his stuff across the aisle, in a quartet of chairs facing each other. Slanting rain began to fall on the glass, and I sat with the soft brown bunny whom I had grown to appreciate mostly because it was not so special, was eminently replaceable in nearly any toy store, and dug out my word search book. As the train pulled from the station, I could peripherally sense the waving hand of my beloved babysitter, her bright and sad smile, those dripping black eyes, but I would never see her again, and I knew it even if she did not, so I began putting loops around various letters into false words to make it difficult to see where the real words were so I could do the searches all over again. She was at the station; I was on the train with a stranger; my mother was somewhere in a white room surrounded by nurses. JKAKLWEL. FSTL. OPTGE.

The conductor walked in through the electric door. "To Los Angeles Union Station," he announced cheerfully, punching my ticket. "Sleeper will be next car down, showers too." He had a belly like a swell of water just contained beneath the buttons of his shirt. "You traveling alone, miss?"

"With me," said the steward, from his spot across the aisle. "She's with me."

The conductor turned. "Not sitting together?"

"No," said the steward. "We are not."

The conductor retucked his shirt into his pants. He took his time setting our tickets just right in their slots. "We're not busy on this stretch," he said, "but you may have to rethink that later. Looks like you have two sleepers," he said, peering at the steward's ticket. "Under eighteen can't be in a sleeper alone."

"Of course not," said the steward. "We will share one."

"And the second?"

"Is for other things," said the steward.

"Like?"

"Luggage."

The conductor stared at him blankly, and the steward raised his eyebrows with an imperiousness, like he always bought two of something, like it was the most normal and middle-class thing in the world to do. Finally, the conductor shrugged, muttered something about coming back by later to check, and went on to the next row.

Once he was far down the aisle and out of hearing range, the steward leaned across. "Whatever you want to do," he whispered, "is fine. Do you want your own sleeper?" I nodded. "Fine," he said. "We'll figure it out. No one's going to check."

I watched his mouth, making words.

"You won't be scared in one by yourself?"

"No."

It was the first word I'd spoken fully aloud to him, and we both could hear the rightness of it.

—

Over the initial hours of the train ride, I continued my word searching, and the steward on and off read a book. Landscape filled the windows, colors rich and fertile as we traversed the center of Oregon, past trickling streams and craggy green cliffsides. We moved through the woodsy towns of Salem and Albany, with riders getting on and off, stations embellished by fine brickwork, hours later passing those billboards advertising Ashland shows that would take place on multiple stages a hundred miles west. This was a famous train ride, I would find out later. The Coast Starlight. It was on people's lists of things to do before they died.

As we went along, I remember a lot of looking out the window, and sometimes turning my gaze down to the puzzle book, fingers circling letters with a pen, but that was the extent of it. The steward took notes from a pile of old books that looked like they'd been left out in a beach house and ruined by the tide. He was there, and I was aware of him there, but I neither trusted nor distrusted him; his was a largely neutral presence that did little to undo my experience of aloneness. Or, my experience of me and the butterfly, the butterfly that had pushed through the lampshade that I was now carrying inside me. Sometimes, he did glance over as if to ensure I was still in my seat, but I barely needed to use the bathroom, or stretch, and sitting very still and breathing shallowly seemed the best way not to jar myself into realizing what was happening. A small motion, as in any motion, released through me an excruciating ripple of understanding, but if I held myself stonelike I could almost keep myself from moving into the knowledge as well.

The train honked, moved through a mountain corridor. Cheerful markers at the sides of the tracks welcomed us to the capital city of Eugene, where someone had stuck a drawing on the station sign of the state bird meadowlark flying in a burst of yellow overhead.

We stayed at the Eugene station for longer than the other stops, and once the train resumed, the steward invited me to join him at the first announced available seating in the dining car. Together, we crossed into a train car small and elegant, with small glass holders on each table set to throw flickering candlelight onto red tablecloths. As we settled into our seats, adults, mostly women, smiled at me, asking the steward if I was his daughter, or little sister. He returned the smiles, silent. "Well, she's a doll," said an older woman in a patterned jacket, passing through to another table. I positioned myself on the side of the table that tracked the scenery gone by, and outside the big picture windows, golden light began to drench the landscape as the sun reached the edge of the horizon. Clinking silverware and jabbered conversation filled the car. When our food arrived, the steward and I ate quietly, as if my uncle had actually told him not to talk to me, and my mind filled with non-thoughts, with blocks of sensation, golden dusk, the sparkle on the water glass, crispy french fry smell, our chuggedy movement down the edge of the land. After dessert, two silver bowls of ice cream, the sun slipping behind the hills, the steward pulled the babysitter's instruction paper from his jacket pocket and read what he could in the dimming pink light.

"It says here your bedtime is eight-thirty," he said. "It's seven-thirty now."

I turned from the window. His eyes were small and dark, the eyelids rough-looking, papery. His mouth, wide, thin, did look a little like my uncle's. He picked up one of his books. "Shall I read aloud?"

It was a mustard yellow book, stained with multiple rings from drinks.

"Whales," he said. "I've been reading this week about whales."

I didn't respond, and he thought about it for a while, then thumbed to the middle somewhere, finding his bookmark. He did not return to the beginning of the book, but began to read, in a quiet voice, a hushed voice that even the table next to us would not be able to hear, where he had left off. I leaned back on my side of the booth. I felt such a tiredness inside me. The butterfly and my thoughts about the butterfly were waiting for me to pore over once I was alone, but the rest of the world was like some kind of swirl, a minute-by-minute negotiation of swirl, my mother swirled inside all of it, and inside the swirl there were small things to hold on to, handrails to find, and the way he was reading was one of them. "The captain stood by the mast of the ship to peer at the shape in the distant water." Outside, the light of evening washed to the palest of blues. The table next to us, two children and two parents, sent a clatter of forks to the floor. "Sssh, Evan, it's a restaurant!" Even at eight years old, there was something in the steward's way of reading that was significant to me. That at first what I heard were words about whales unattached to any story or context, and therefore easy to listen to, without any bait inside them. I did not have the energy to care about a book, and to start at the beginning might have felt a demand on my attention, but to start where he had left off meant he would be fully engaged and I could drift in and out as needed, could conserve everything else inside me to maintain the moment-by-moment human operation. This tiny choice he made, this delicate calibration of his position against mine, of our two-peopleness. The chapter was about a whale that had injured a fin and had been attended to by a series of divers off the coast of Australia. The blue outside intensified, and later, when I would think back on that moment, which I think about not infrequently, hearing his voice, imagining us rolling through the evening landscape, inside the blackness of the tent, I can see the darkening shadows of trees and houses blurring into whale pods and divers and schools of darting fish.

He read for a half hour or so as people moved in and out of the dining car, and I drifted in and out, too, and then for the remaining time he waved off the waiter and we just looked together out the window at the silhouetted shapes of the small trackside towns.

At 8:15, we returned to our sitting car, and he took down my rolly suitcase, found my toothbrush in my bag and a red washcloth I hadn't remembered packing, and stood outside the bathroom door while I did my getting ready. At the sleeper, he asked if he could step inside and then scouted around until he found an embedded light by a higher bunk that looked suitably dim. "This okay?" "Yes. Thank you." I would turn it off once he left. He said the second sleeper was right next door and he would go in there now and all I had to do was knock or even tap the wall if I needed anything, anything at all. "I sleep very lightly," he said, "and my ears are good. If you need me at any moment," he said, "just tap. Okay?" "Okay." "Should we do a practice run?" "No, it's all right." "You feel comfortable?" "I do." "Good night then, Francie." "Good night."

By then, I could feel the tears gathering inside again, the way the clouds internal attached to one another several times a day, gathering into something physical to shed, so I began to close the door on him and he allowed himself to be shuttled out. I did not soften the crying, could not, but I did it in the farthest corner from his I could find, into the roughness of a gray woolen train blanket, and he neither knocked nor ever commented.

After I was done and had changed into my nightgown, I lay on the lumpy little cot and pulled the woolen blanket over me. The train bumped along the tracks. I had slide-locked the door, and yanked the flimsy yellow curtains over the window, and turned off the light, and with my body in the bed, arms wrapped around the negligible brown bunny, I let my mind relax and finally take its natural course which was to return to thoughts about the butterfly. I did not want to think about my mother, and don't remember having any conscious thoughts of her at that moment. On the cot, in the tent, memory creating its own new glint in my mind, instead I replayed the moment in the babysitter's apartment again and again: the shade with its tour of golden butterflies, the magic miracle hiding in the group, the strong sensation of pulling, the flash view of the butterfly floating, and finally the swallowing of the full glass of water with the butterfly rafting down my throat and into the darkness inside.

Only then, in the dim half-quiet of the sleeper with the sounds of other travelers moving back and forth through the train cars outside my door, the loud button-pushing of the bathroom door, the vacuum of the flush, scraps of chatty conversation between strangers laughing about the difficulty of passing through tight quarters, did I think of the paper from the school front lawn, the paper with the beetle test on it that I had picked up just a couple days earlier, an era ago, and had so carefully folded and tucked into the small pocket of my knapsack. The bag was right there on the floor at the base of the cot, and I pulled it up onto the woolen blanket. What were the chances, really, that the one paper that had been left out on the lawn would be a paper with pictures of bugs on it? Out of all the possible papers in all the backpacks belonging to all the children of the various grades? And I had not passed it by, either—that paper had drawn me to it like it had flung hooks and claws into my skin, and there is nothing I can imagine outside of floods and bombings that would've stopped me from running over and picking it up and taking it home. I knew it was mine from all the way across the lawn, the same way I knew that lamp was mine as soon as I stepped into the babysitter's apartment.

A flutter of fear moved inside me then, holding the backpack, waiting and watching the zipped pocket, like even with the zipper closed I might see lines of antennae beginning to peek out as the beetle dropped off the paper, the beetles, the clicking legs and bodies, and my destiny ahead of me, the feeling like it was out of my hands, this life of mine, and there were things in it pointed at me that I could not unpoint. Two begins a pattern. I did not know if anything had actually emerged in there, but I still could feel the weight of the moment, the revving of those subterranean gears, my own tense lip and jaw and the clacking of the tracks as we moved through towns and villages where people lived in houses going about their lives, inside their own bodies, all of us in our compartments, the steward in his own next door reading a book.

All I could do was hold the bag. To open the pocket right then would have been the action of a different person. I held it close, next to the stuffed bunny, and like so many travelers before me, over decades and various terrains, in books and in life, the pressure of soft things and the clickety-clack of a train lulled me fast to sleep.

51

Vicky stirs on the couch. I rise up out of it, wait. The traffic light changes downstairs. The roads are, by now, mostly quiet. I am on the edge of something. Don't wake up, I think at her, don't you wake up, Vicky. Sleep, stay sleeping. I won't hurt you. Don't come. In the loft with the babysitter so many years before, I had heard her fall asleep and had felt her leave the room with her wakeful mind, and she had been alive and asleep at the same time, and it meant something to me, then, to be in the same space with someone alive and asleep, all at once comforted and abandoned. She releases a sigh, resettles herself. The couch cushions loosen. Wheels roll through the city.

52

Hours later, sometime in the night, there was a knock at the door of my sleeper car. I had been deep asleep, soothed by the forward motion of the train, dreaming about some kind of river, a cold-weather rocky river, with fish hitting the rocks and flipping up in the air, when my body started awake, hard, as if I were one of the fish and had just hit a rock. The sound, before it attached to anything real, was just this pounding, this floating loud pounding coming from all sides, shaking the walls before it solidified and settled itself at my door, shaped and smaller, performed by a hand.

I was groggy and half-asleep, and the easiest choice was to respond to the summons, so I got out of bed, found the door of the sleeper, and opened it.

A gust of cold air blew in from the corridor. In the hallway, wrapped in a jacket, stood a woman in a dark suit, wearing a dark hat, holding a piece of paper. She was an adult. I did not know her. She was powerfully ordinary-looking. Easily balanced and indistinct in her features. I had no idea what time it was—if it was the middle of the night or a time still suitable for adult awakeness.

"Hello!" she said, looking down at me. "Excuse me. I'm sorry to wake you. Do you have a paper?"

I frowned at her. "A paper?" I said. "What do you mean?"

"A paper?" she said. She consulted her own piece of paper.

Next door, the steward opened up. "Excuse me? Can I help you?"

"I am looking," the woman said, turning to him, "for a paper."

He stepped forward to block her like a football player, as if she was going to march right into my sleeper and tackle me. But she barely responded; she was so primly held inside her clothes. Her hair so rightly in place it didn't look like hair, but more like marker drawn in thick lines on a skull.

"What sort of paper?"

She consulted her paper again. "I don't know," she said. She looked back up at us both and smiled brightly. "Excuse me," she said. "It seems I need more information. I apologize for waking you up."

"Are you sure you picked the right car?"

She nodded. "Yes," she said, holding on to her smile. "That part is correct. I do apologize again."

"And what is your name?" asked the steward, but she'd already turned away. She clicked off down the car and through the intermediary door.

The steward turned to me. He was wearing gray flannel pajamas and his eyes looked even smaller and more mole-like woken up. "You okay?"

"Yes."

"A paper? She wanted a paper?"

"I don't know. That's what she said."

"We can ask the conductor tomorrow. They shouldn't have people knocking on sleepers at midnight! You sure you're okay?"

"Yes."

"Your room fine?" he asked.

"Yes."

He stood there. "Go back to bed. I'll wait here for a little bit. I'll guard the door."

"I wasn't scared."

"Even so," he said. "I'll be here. I'm here if you need me."

He settled himself at my door and watched me climb back into my bunk. But his presence there meant the light from the corridor came streaming in, and the wind of velocity from the movement of the train rattled loudly, and the room grew colder, fast, until finally I told him that I'd lock it behind him and I promised I wouldn't open it again if anyone else knocked.

He nodded, with reluctance.

"You wouldn't like me to stay inside and sit on the other bunk—?"

"No," closing the door.

We spoke with the conductor very early the following morning, but no one else had made a report of a woman tapping on sleeper cars in the middle of the night asking for a piece of paper. She did not match the description of anyone he had seen on the train. The conductor, upon my inquiry, said my mother had not called on the emergency train line or the conductor's personal cellular phone to find out the room assignments, so it was not somehow related to her. "I'll keep an eye out," the conductor said, scratching his forehead, and the steward thanked him several times. "A dark hat," he called as we walked away, "like something from a movie." As we settled back into our non-sleeper seats, the sun had newly risen, and through the thin gray light I watched the people board at the Emeryville station, a fresh influx of riders tucking their suitcases above the seats and into the special aisle areas. I told the steward again that I had not been scared. "All she wanted was paper," I said. "No big deal." It was only right then, on the train, in the tent, looking out at a short man kissing a woman goodbye against the distant shadowed brown bluffs of the Northern Californian landscape, saying it aloud, that I made the connection to the paper in my backpack, the one with the beetles on it that I had not yet been able to check.

I didn't speak to the steward during breakfast, and when he continued to read aloud from his whale book, I stared out the window and recounted the experience of it to myself again: her knock, her face, the inadequate information.

We got off the train in Salinas and tried calling my mother at my request from a phone booth at the station. On the other line, the nurse went to check and I stayed on hold for five minutes while passengers bought muffins from nearby stands, standing in line for coffee, sipping, chatting, the steward outside the phone booth standing straight and still. After some time, the nurse returned to the phone line and said not yet. "It's important we go slow here," she said, softly. "I'm so sorry." I stayed quiet on the line until the nurse said, "Hello?" and then I hung up. The steward examined my face and asked if I would like a snack, as he had some cash my uncle had given him, and even though it was morning I requested a hot dog and he purchased two at a nearby cart which we ate on a bench in a half-garden at the back of the station where some old tomato plants grew in scraggly vines by the edge of the dirt. The sun stretched its pale morning color over the grasslands by the nearby houses. We were now over halfway there, the steward told me, chewing his hot dog, which he had piled high with pickle relish and mustard. There were beautiful garlic farms off to the south, he pointed. I asked him if he liked working for the train, and he wiped his mouth and smiled out to the world and said he didn't work for the train, that he was a graduate student, and he was able to join me because it was spring break and he had the week off from courses. He dabbed a dot of mustard off his cheek with a napkin, and the dot moved from his face onto the napkin, where it would soon voyage to the trash. Everything forever in motion. He explained that he would be visiting a library in Pasadena that had some books he needed to consult, and then once he had done his research, he would fly home. After I was settled. My uncle would be picking me up at the station.

I turned to look at him. Why, I asked, did he have a jacket with a train on it if he did not work for the train?

He laughed. "You noticed that?" he said. "I'm so glad. I dug it out of my closet on Friday when your uncle explained the job. I bought it years ago. I thought it was a neat coincidence."

Something about it was bad, but it all was bad, and so I stopped eating my hot dog and threw it and its pleated paper boat into the trash can to live the rest of its existence with the mustard dot on his napkin and all the previous train customer waste. In the near distance, a gaunt bearded man walked with a plastic bag, picking up loose trash with a poker stick. "Boarding!" called the conductor, and as a breeze passed through the ragged leaves of the tomato plant, we abandoned our debris, and moved our bodies elsewhere. All of it felt so frighteningly familiar, the car pickup line all over again, me and my mother different flashing points on a map moving farther apart by the minute, stretched away from each other, and back on board, a rush of sour courage seemed to move through me, rancid, and urgent, and once we were seated and the train was in motion again, I reached under my seat and pulled out the purple knapsack.

"Please," I said, pushing it toward the steward. I pointed to the small pocket.

"You want me to open that?" He unzipped it. "What do you need?"

"I want to know what's in there."

He rummaged around. "A few pens? Some paper?"

"A bug?"

He yanked his hand out and laughed with surprise. "A bug?"

"A beetle?"

"An alive beetle?"

"Or maybe two?"

"Seriously?" he said.

"Pull out the white paper. The folded white paper," I said. "Please." I was leaning in, speaking louder than usual, biting down on the words. It was, by far, the most involved conversation I'd had yet with him. He pressed in his lips, and with caution, used two fingers to tug the paper out by its edge.

"You mean this?"

"Will you open it?"

"Are there bugs in there?"

"I don't know."

He held the paper in his fingers like a dirty cloth, and with the other hand zipped the small pocket back up and put the knapsack on the floor. By that point, it was clear that the paper he was holding was just a paper, with nothing sticking out of it, or tucked inside, but when he lifted the edge to open, to show me the interior, it revealed itself to be blank. How can I convey this, even to myself? The paper was not entirely blank, not even mostly blank, but more blank than it had been before, now with two printed drawings of beetles in two separate boxes and the third, the one at the bottom, empty. In that one, the beetle illustration was gone, lines still radiating from the square with the student's wobbly handwriting labeling parts no longer there. The train hurtled forward, and the conductor moved through our aisle to clip new tickets. With effort, I asked the steward to hand me the knapsack, please, thank you, the words of politeness a template to cling to right then, anchors to the world of the regular, and he gave it back, shaking his head and laughing a little and going down the aisle to the restroom to wash his hands. A light wind passed through the railroad car. Two women, far at the other end, burst into laughter. He had left the piece of folded paper on the pullout dining tray, and while he was out of view, I picked it up by a corner, fingers trembling. The paper had no more purpose for me, was only the carcass now, the empty shell, so I fed it through a slot of open window, watching as it blew past the iron railroad ties, fluttering to the ground. Maybe it would find that woman, wherever she was. Maybe she could track its history better than I could. I watched it tumble on the rocks for a few minutes until it was out of sight, and then I shouldered the knapsack and went to wash my own hands.

The steward found me outside the bathroom and asked if I was okay, said I looked pale, and he told me if I wanted to rest I could always return to the sleeper. Or rest in my chair. He was not tired. He would be near. Was there anything about that paper he'd lifted out? he asked. Did I, was it the paper you think the woman was looking for last night? I didn't reply, but he looked away, his eyebrows pulling in, pained, and as gently and kindly as he could he said that he didn't think the woman would be out and about late in the night looking for my homework. "I just don't think that was the paper she meant," he said. "I'm sorry." The train moved through a tunnel, darkening. It was difficult right then for the steward to meet my eyes, but not for me to stay with his; I had him in my sights by then, his adulthood and reasoning, noting that well-worn gap between us, the "someone" blanket gap, between the world of rational thinkers and the rest. He was a man who went to graduate school and attended libraries and read about whales. I felt a kind of power over him then, and told him yes, it was a good idea, that I would go to the sleeper for a little while, and I walked down the rows of cars with the knapsack close on my back, train car windows exposing daylight again, him following quietly behind me so as not to disturb me with his presence.

The light in the sleeper was a raw afternoon yellow, the curtain still pulled. I lay down on the cot and listened to the train move below me for a while. I had a task to do, and I was carrying it in my mind as surely as if it were a solid thing, but for now I was waiting. As if on schedule, the tears surged up, and I cried them out into the same rough gray woolen blanket to get them out of the way. The nurse's concerned voice on the phone. My mother unable to talk. A woman laughing outside the sleeper door about cubicles. Some kid feet running. I can't do it, I thought to myself, wiping my eyes, knowing I would do it. I sat up on the cot and pulled the knapsack into my lap. I did not want to see it first; I wanted my hand to see it first, so I closed my eyes. The dark, as before, helped me: the dark where I felt myself more clearly, the dark of my bedroom with no night-light. My heart started beating in my throat, and I groped over the knapsack to find the zipper of the small pocket, used the metal tab to split the fabric open, and reached my hand inside.

Next door, the steward, most likely, was back on his own cot, reading his book. I could almost feel him quietly reading, studying, the other people on the train, the train arriving at Union Station in seven more hours, soon to pass through the golden-blue radiance of San Luis Obispo and the massive sea-bathed rocks of Morro Bay, which I would see once I was back in my seat, dazed, eyes glued to the window. My hand moved around in the pocket, reaching slowly to the bottom, progressing past the pens and their smooth slim plastic cylinders, past a couple pen caps, separated from the pen bodies, down to the crevices of canvas. The canvas had a fraying sewn hem rimming the edge of the pocket, and my fingers started at the far corner and moved along the border, and it did not take long to make contact. The thing was solid, and delicate, and unmoving. I touched the shape of it, an oval, sticks protruding from the sides. Felt the smoothness of its backside, and the extended stag antlers. A beetle. What seemed to be a dead beetle. I lifted it out by the end of one of its legs and placed it into my palm, and with eyes still closed, for a while just sat there with it resting in my hand.

It isn't easy to name what I felt; as a child, I was immersed in feeling without name, and in the memory tent, trying to capture it, the best word I could summon up for myself was resigned. It was here. It was asserting its presence entirely. I could feel its small weight and deadness in my hand. It was a thing, now. It could not be denied. When I finally opened my eyes, it was by then an afterthought, only to add color. I had run my fingers over it for many minutes and knew its shape and size well. The sun had gone behind a cloud, and in the now grayish light of the sleeper car, it looked only black, though years later, when I would show it to Vicky, dazzling sun streaming in from my bedroom window from a cloudless valley sky, the daylight and angle revealed a dark red shimmer glow, and she, crouched by my side, four or five years old, had gasped at its beauty.

I held it for some time, then put it back into my small knapsack pocket and zipped it closed.

53

We tried my mother at the pay phone in Santa Barbara, and at the pay phone in Oxnard, but each time the nurse said she was either seeing the doctor or resting. The steward's cell phone did not work well on the train due to his payment plan, and the train itself at that time had spotty reception. "Tell her it's Francie," I told the nurse, and she said she understood the importance, but that she was reporting the truth. "She might be out on the floor in the late afternoon," she said, scratching a pen against something hard. "Try again then. There's a better chance then."

We were closing in on Southern California by this point, and the steward and I spent the rest of the trip largely in our seats before the big city entered our view. He continued to read his books, and to give my mind a break from the shock of the butterfly and now the beetle, the inert feeling of the beetle body and its delicate legs split at the joint still a vivid ghost memory on the palm of my hand, I went through the different puzzles in my word search book again. I tried to fill in any of the leftover clues on crosswords I hadn't been able to figure out, which was most of them. I found the wrong items in a park scene, including a teacup in a tree. I made a puppy's face by linking a series of dots. With every scratch of the pencil, the odor of pale brown newsprint released to the air, and later, even a whiff of those newsprint game books found at stations of any kind would raise up in me a vicious wave of nausea. It was becoming, to me, the precise smell of dislocation. When I raised my head to look outside the window, the ocean had grown lighter, a frothy blue, and the houses out the other side were larger, whiter, more imposingly moneyed. The steward and I ventured to the snack car to have cheese puffs and grape juice, and the steward pointed out the slow black curve of a dolphin fin rising from the surface of rolling waves. Riders exited, and new people came on at Ventura with their bags and purses to find and settle into seats.

I was back in my spot, looking out the window, glad that the older woman who had been sitting near me trying to chat me up with polite, concerned questions had disembarked, and the steward was working his pencil over a yellow legal pad with an elbow lodged in an open book to hold the page, when a man in a black suit walked through the doors at the far end of our train car.

He was a striking man. Tall, with slick black hair

just visible under a hat, acne-scarred skin, a prominent nose, and the suit. It was hard not to take notice of him. He looked a lot like the male version of the woman who had knocked on my door the night before. My memory of him, up until now, had been vague, but in the tent, he was sharp, and clear.

He passed through the length of the car and came to a stop at our end, where he turned on his heel and faced me.

"Tickets," he said, standing at the edge of the seat next to mine.

I pointed across the aisle to the steward, who rummaged in his pocket. "You're not the usual ticket-taker," he said.

"No," said the man.

Silence stretched between the three of us. Our tickets were wedged up on the metal ridge above the seats, anyway—we'd had to show them only the first day, upon settling in, and every successive pass-through our usual ticket-taker gave us a knowing nod as he walked by.

"I already gave them to the conductor," said the steward, patting his jacket. "I just realized."

The man stood there. His shoes shone; his eyebrows rested thick and sturdy against a pale, sweatless forehead.

"Tickets," he said.

"I'm sorry," said the steward. "We have no tickets."

The man rotated to face me again, and behind

him, I could see the steward rise from his seat with his long brittle arms and legs to scuttle over to my side of the aisle to be my protector. But I had not been afraid of the woman, and I was not afraid of this man, this lunkish man who kept repeating himself. I was interested. He reminded me of something.

He turned his strong dark eyes back on me.

"Tickets," he said.

"We already gave them away," I said.

"Tickets," he said, and behind the darkness in his gaze I could now glimpse a small measure of pleading.

I wasn't sure what to do, but something was shifting in my perception of what was happening, and it was so slippery I could barely grasp it, but I could, I could catch a tiny hold on a string coming out of the moment, to pull it in, to see. Based on where he was standing, and his suit, and his formality, he seemed to be making a request for our tickets; that is what usually happened on a train. He was performing all of those functions, albeit wrongly. But as I was sitting there, I understood, in a most basic way, that he was actually asking us for his. That we were a source for him, that he was looking to us to supply him. I had no tickets, and I was neither conductor nor ticket booth, but in order to do something, I reached down into the purple drawstring bag at my feet, into the larger pocket. Near the top were some ripped pieces of paper left over from drawings I had started the day before and quickly grown tired of, and I pulled one of them out and tore the paper into two jaggedy rectangles, folding down the rough edges. The tall man watched me do the work. He watched with a great care and focus. I remember feeling then, in the depth of his watching, that without knowing what I looked like, he had been searching specifically for me. I took a pencil and wrote TICKET in capitals on one piece of paper, and TICKET in capitals on the next, thickening the letters by going over them a few times. Behind the word, a whorl of crayon movement and parts of bird wings and cat heads.

"Here," I said. I handed the pieces of paper over to the man.

The steward was perched on the armrest of the seat across from me, poised for any quick action. But the tall man moved slowly. He straightened up to his full height and his dark eyes scanned the papers I had given him. He looked at them for what seemed to be a long time, deeply searching them with his gaze, before tucking them both into the front pocket of his suit jacket. He bowed a little to me, and then walked directly to the door that separated the cars, pressed the rectangular button to open, and exited.

The steward went to the door and watched through the small window. After a few minutes, he returned to tell me the man had walked through the entire subsequent car and gone through the door at that end as well.

"Well!" said the steward, sitting fully back into a seat. A light sheen of sweat framed his brow. "Well done. That was a little strange, huh? Do you think it was related to the other night? Who was that man?"

I closed my drawstring bag. Stored the pencil back inside the word search book.

"He wanted tickets," I said.

"But was there something off about him? He looked so put together."

"I'm going to the bathroom," I said.

"I'll wait at the door." The steward returned to the window between cars. "No sign of him. You're good."

Like the previous night with the woman visitor, the steward worrying in the doorframe, I felt, for a second, the strain of him there, this protective, good steward, shepherding me.

"He was not off," I said. "He was on."

I used the bathroom, and then did something I had not done in the two days of the trip so far, which was to, by my own volition, go up and down our train car. As I walked the carpeted row I saw for the first time the other people also traveling with us in their seats, doing their reading or typing or sleeping, and the various shades and shapes of hair and skin and shoes and hands and phones and the wavy stripes of blue and brown landscape rushing past as we moved inland. The steward watched me carefully. I went to the end and rose on my tiptoes and also looked myself through the window separating the cars.

"I'd like to go look for him," I said, turning to the steward.

"The man? That strange man?"

"Please."

Together, we wended through the chain of cars, me leading the way through each metal segment, including the dining car, which was empty of people and table dressings in between meals, and the first-class car with its red seats and pointy-toed shoes, and the movie car with the uplifted televisions that were hard to see with the bands of daylight moving into the room even under and around the pulled shades. We walked until we reached the front of the train, with the conductor in his sunglasses leaning back in some kind of special chair, talking to a customer, and when the man with the suit and hat was not to be found, we turned around and tailed the train all the way to its other end, bumping and jiggling along the route the whole time.

"He must be in the bathroom," said the steward, once we'd reached the end.

I nodded, but only as an actor nods on a stage according to script, because I knew, and I imagined in some way the steward knew, that the man in the suit, like the woman in the suit, was gone.

54

For the last portion of the ride, the steward and I went to the Sightseer Lounge to watch the city rising and squaring itself before us. Through the patches of fresh air coming in from the intermediary gaps, we could smell the grime and exhaust while glimpsing miniature cars on freeways in winding, glittering lines. We were only one stop from downtown Los Angeles by now and while angling in from the valley glimpsed in the far distance the rise of apartment buildings and the graffiti of indecipherable spiky letters scratched on walls, and skyscrapers off to the east that rose silver into a strobe-lit sky. Honking bleats, and the shifting black dots of birds.

The final stop before Union Station was Burbank. At the pay phone, the nurse connected me directly to my mother.

"Honey," my mother said. Her voice sounded thin, tremulous. "Where are you?"

"Burbank." I gripped the receiver.

"They said you're taking the train?"

"I'm in Burbank," I said, reading the large white plastic letters on the gray archway in front of me.

"You're off the train?"

"Not yet. We're taking it to the end so it isn't rushed."

"Francie. It's so good to hear you. When I'm better, we'll go to Disneyland together. I'll come right down and see you, okay? I'll get well, and when I'm really good you'll come back here to be with me again and we'll play cards all day and have ice cream every meal. Okay?"

The steward was standing under one of the gray archways, watching the planes taking off in unusually sharp angles from the nearby airport.

"Your aunt is a wonderful person," my mother said, after the loud rumble of plane passed. "You'll be in very good hands." She started to cry.

The wind passed through the station to ruffle the meadow grasses over by the rail lines.

"There's a dining car," I said.

"On the train?"

"Yes."

"Is the food good?"

"The food is fine."

"Who are you with?"

"A man."

"Uncle Stan?"

"No. A stranger man."

"Not Aunt Minn?"

"Aunt Minn had the baby."

"Of course. Of course she did. Please, Francie. What's his name?"

"I don't know."

"Is he nice?"

"Yes."

"He's being nice to you? All the time?"

"Yes."

"Is he nearby?"

"Yes."

"Will you put him on the phone?" The tears were streaking down her face; I could picture them clearly from the way she was sniffing. An assortment of machines beeped behind her. Above us, another plane rose noisily, and I waved at the steward, who came over and took the phone from my hands. "She's crying," I said. He hunched close to the receiver like Uncle Stan had, so long ago on the steps of the elementary school, and in a low but audible voice the steward also reported information about my eating and sleeping and how I was doing well in spite of the circumstances. I heard him explaining how he was a second cousin on Uncle Stan's side, and a graduate student on a break from classes. "She's very capable," he said.

The conductor poked his head out of the front car and waved us on. "Pulling anchor in one minute!" he called. The steward said goodbye to my mother, and I followed him back on. From our train car, portions of the airport were visible—large hangars, vast and flat parking lots for planes of all sizes, the misspelled sign I would read so many times in my future at the 165 bus stop down Vanowen stating **passanger pickup**. Cement blocks by the side of the road sheltered by waving stalks of grass.

"Union Station!" said the conductor, plucking our paper tickets from the seats.

Forty-five minutes later, upon arrival, while the steward handled my black rolly bag and I wore my purple knapsack, him herding us in the right direction, I kept my eyes on the ground, looking for what might be considered ticket stubs as possibly used by the man in the suit. I checked on the windows, sidewalk, and stairs. As we walked beneath the high ceilings of Union Station, through the shining brown galleries and pews, the intricate tiled floors and geometric paneling, I saw a pigeon trying to peck at a scrap of paper that looked like it might have once had part of my drawing on it. I thought I recognized the orange lines of a half-hearted one-color rainbow. People sped by in whispery flutters of clothing and the pigeon, gray, dull, hungry, looking exactly like every other pigeon I'd ever seen, abandoned the paper on the ground and went off to investigate a more promising bit of potato chip. I did not point out the scrap to the steward, who was trying to find my uncle's information in all his various papers, and the wind from the movement of people's quickening feet blew the orange scraps away, anyway, toward the open side doors, leading to the Metro. The steward and I walked side by side toward the line of taxis together, to Uncle Stan, who was waiting for me as promised in his Orioles cap. The sky of the city of Los Angeles was bigger and wider and a faint purpled-gray color, even at night. The invisible baton reached from the steward's hand to my uncle's and I stood at his side as they shook hands and completed the pass. The steward turned to me and bent down and reached out a hand to clasp mine, to look me in the eye and wish me well, and then he pivoted on his heel and disappeared behind us into the flow of walkers.

55

"How was the trip?" asked Uncle Stan, taking my hand as we walked toward the parking lot.

"Fine."

"Did you see amazing sights?"

"Just what was out the window."

"I'm so excited for you to meet Vicky," he said. "She's tiny! She's this tiny thing!"

We found his car in the parking lot—blue, small, shiny—and he popped the trunk and put my rolly bag inside. I kept ahold of my purple knapsack.

Once we were settled into the seats, me on a booster next to a giant plaid car seat facing backward, him at the wheel, he turned to face me. "Welcome, Francie," he said, and his eyes grew wet. "We are very glad you are here." He started the car. We drove on the freeways to his home, the red and yellow lights stretching and shortening as I slivered my eyes. I remember picturing the apartment in Portland right then, on the drive, the five rooms with no one in them. I knew I would not be returning, and it would take weeks for it all to be cleaned out and ready to rent to someone new. Where would my toys and schoolwork go? To Goodwill, I thought. Around the corner. Had anyone told Alberta not to pick me up? They had my booster in their car. Who would handle my mother's clothes and perfumes? It was all spread in bits, like the trash we had left in Salinas, this life rubble. Someone would clean up my toys and another girl would buy my dolls and love them, likely more than I had. Another might trim the plants in the front of the building and find a kabob skewer, use it on a grill. Once it was all cleaned up, and sorted, and sold, and rerouted, the entire history of the life with my mother would be undocumented except on some old cassette tapes that would soon crumble to dust.

56

At the door of their house, before I began my new life, I realized that the beetle and the butterfly had likely been the tickets. Which would mean that I was also a ticket, because one of those was inside me. I had the thought, and then I forgot it.

Behind me, Uncle Stan popped the trunk. He pulled out my bag. "Here we are!" he said. "Your new home!" He fumbled with his keys.

The air was lighter here, hotter, even at night. All the colors different. Lawns of clipped grass blades. The tire swing across the street. I heard footsteps moving down a staircase indoors.

"Francie," I said, pointing to myself, when Aunt Minn opened the door, the baby in her arms.

PART FIVE

Rose

57

The morning after the sleepover, Vicky and I go to brunch down the street, at a large windowed diner with cutouts of movie scenes under the glass on the tabletops. Seemingly overnight, the weather shifted to a real Southern Californian fall, the dry, crisping heat of October over. There's a fresh streak of cold in the air, and we're wearing our sweatshirts and socks.

In the very early morning, Vicky woke up with the sun as I have no curtains, skipped into my room, and found me there, in bed, awake. I had slept a little, in the late hours, after the long visit to the tent, after the return to my bed, and some tears. "You did it!" she crowed. "Francie! You did it!" She crawled into bed with me, knocked again on her skull.

"I'm alive!" she called out, hooting.

She got up to dance around the room, and I watched her, smiling, laughing as she kicked and spun, as she raised my arm high like a welterweight champ, but the memories in the tent had been so concentrated that I had nearly forgotten the original purpose of the visit. Vicky was marching through the hall, singing, and said we had to go celebrate, so we threw on layers and headed out to walk to the diner down the street. She linked her arm in mine. I could feel, on my arm, the full breathing warmth of her.

After we sat down and the waiter took our order, I filled her in a little bit about some of what I remembered—about her father picking me up, about the drive from Union Station to their house, our house. About the steward disappearing into the masses of people, never to be seen again. The details are sad, but she says she can still see that something was helpful over the course of the night, can locate a slightly different look on my face, what she calls a washed-out look, but good washed-out, not like old washed-out. Washed clear, she says. Over her stack of blueberry pancakes, she asks if I had had any desire to hurt her, and I say no, it had been different than I'd expected. "See? See?" she says, waving a forkful of pancake in the air. She asks if I'm done with Jose now, and I laugh and tell her no, of course not. Though I keep to myself how something hard to identify about his purpose may have shifted a little in my mind. I don't tell her much else about what I remembered—just that there was a man in a suit and a woman in a suit looking for things, and they seemed like they came from another place, or were speaking in another language that was still pretending to be our language, and I hadn't recalled some of the key details about them until last night with her there, nearby, asleep, and that in some tenuous way they were important to me. "I'll tell you more later," I say. "I'm still figuring it out." She nods, finishes her orange juice. "I slept weirdly well," she says. "On that brick of a couch." She beams at me, with her golden-fringed eyes. Her face ready, and happy. Everything about her is a radiant portrait of health, but she is almost the age that can begin to be fragile, the time to watch carefully for those with the genetic load of mental fragility, the heightened era. College. She seems like she will be just fine. I have never allowed myself to worry. I sip my coffee and look out the window.

Once she's home and settled, and I've reinstalled the lock on my bedroom door and chatted with Jose in the hallway about the enjoyment of the morning off, but how we will resume as usual, I go on the computer and for the first time decide to do a search for the name of the babysitter. Not to go see her. Just to consider contacting her. To see if she might remember me. Possibly to thank her. I never ended up visiting her on any of my trips to Portland—her loft was not near my mother's facility, and I avoided the elementary school entirely because I did not feel like returning. My elementary school class did send me one card/note covered with stickers and balloon drawings, which I looked at for about five minutes over a bag of corn chips in the Burbank kitchen before tossing it into the trash. While online, I also try to locate the steward, but the identifying information I have on him is scarce, and possibly he is Stuart, but that reveals little, and Uncle Stan and his cousin Tony are still not speaking, twenty years later, and I don't want to get in the middle of any of that. The steward, for the moment, falls into the map and disappears, and from what I can tell, the possible babysitter's social media identities look to be on private or locked settings.

Only a few objects need wrapping or packing since Vicky helped so much the day before, so with the extra time, I put in a quick call to my mother and ask her how the oldies-but-goodies sing-along went, "well, extremely well!" and hear about her weekend plans with Edward, and how they plan to go early together to the annual Veterans Day parade to cheer on two of the older residents who are walking. When we're off the phone, I do a bit of online responding to interested buyers and future customers who want to double-check item dimensions and color fidelity. The evening is quiet, including a bowl of pasta and the light cleaning of countertops and windowpanes.

But on Monday morning, early, instead of the tent time, for a change, I put in a call to the elementary school. It is listed under the same name, with the same address, and it is, amazingly, the same head secretary, Mrs. Washington, still pert and warm-voiced, who picks up the phone and does a fairly believable job of claiming she remembers me. I ask if her brother is still driving the train in Atlanta, and she said he retired, but her nephew now paints trains and builds them out of found wood and has an exciting exhibit upcoming in New Orleans. We talk about that for a little while, and then when there's a pause I explain to her that the reason I'm calling is that I'm doing a small personal history project, a kind of non-family family tree, and does she happen to have any information about a former babysitter of mine named Shrina who had also worked there at the school as a teacher's aide for some time? I unfortunately do not know her last name. Mrs. Washington, call me Angie, she says, says she might, give her a few minutes and she'll get back to me shortly, and in an hour returns my call with a list of possible emails. "One of these ought to work," she says, laughing at my sounds of surprise, "and please, will you send along a hello from me, too? Wasn't she just terrific?" Then she tells me how I might not even recognize the school now; they painted it a putty color that nobody likes, and revitalized the climbing structures, and the principal is encouraging a new approach to math, which has all the grown-ups scrambling to keep up. "The kids, of course, are fine," she laughs, again. "But I'll just be keeping with my columns, thank you very much."

After we hang up, I stay sitting on the floor for a little while. The carpet is warm from a stretched morning sunspot. Flies buzz against the balcony's screen.

58

Dear Shrina,

Hello. I don't know if you remember me, but many years ago you were very helpful at a difficult point in my life. I wanted to thank you for your kindness and help at such a complicated transition. Even though I was having trouble grasping what was going on, I have been thinking a lot about it, and I have these clear memories of your loft, and the vanilla soy milk, and the fringy scarf. You could not have known how comforting it was to me that you had such a clean and functional kitchen sink drying rack. Are you still a teacher? A babysitter? Do you still have Hattie? I hope so, even though I know that's probably impossible. Maybe Hattie 2? I got your email from Mrs. Washington from the front office, who also sends along a hello. I would love to hear from you if you ever feel comfortable writing back. Thank you again.

Sincerely,
Francie M

59

In those very early morning hours of the sleepover, Vicky came into my room, hooting and laughing.

"You did it!" she crowed, dancing around the room. "I'm alive!"

It is only later, alone, screwing the bolts back into the door, that it occurs to me that the real reason I lock the door might just be because then someone else needs to unlock it.

60

When the roses had arrived under Deena's curtains, I did not jump right away to remembering the man and the woman in the suits; for whatever reason, they had largely slipped my mind as they'd slipped the train, and I had not been able to picture them clearly again until the arrival of the memory tent and its slow, measured movement through time. Instead, what they had imprinted on my brain was a strong desire to take the train again, and after that appearance of the roses, after Vicky claimed hers, and the trash truck took the rest, I was able to convince my uncle to go with me on a day trip via Amtrak to San Diego via the Surfliner to check out the new chimp exhibit at the famous zoo. My uncle was usually up for adventures and loved the idea, and we had a fine day together at Balboa Park, laughing at the chimps and the bears, riding back with the sunset displaying itself in full magnificence against military beaches and nuclear reactors. Nothing happened on the way there, and as the train moved north, bringing us home, I kept glancing at the separating doors and excusing myself to the bathroom. My uncle asked, joking, if I was expecting anyone, or anything, and I laughed for a second, unsure how to answer. Was I? When we got home, I felt overcome with dissatisfaction and, before bed, went to dig out the purple knapsack from the depths of my closet, pushed to a far corner, full still of word searches and tape recorders. I dug around in the small pocket past the pens and the pen caps to find, once again, the beetle. It was dry, almost calcified. One of its legs had broken off. I slept with it on my nightstand, and in the morning, after breakfast, before Vicky came home from a sleepover, I slipped it into my pocket and walked a few blocks to the corner to take the 183 bus up Magnolia toward the mountains. I rode in the back, and when it seemed like a good moment, dropped the beetle down the side of the seat where it fell, half-hidden by some old paper napkins. No one came by. No suits, no glances. I rode the route for a while until the bus was empty, all the way to the end of the line, and then crossed the street and took another one home.

61

After I send the note to the babysitter, I stay on the computer and make a plan to fly up to see my mother again before the winter holidays. I will be spending the actual break time with Vicky and Aunt Minn and Uncle Stan, but I want to give her that silk scarf I found, and a pair of vintage shell-shaped earrings studded with rhinestones that remind me of the pair she wore long ago at Grandma's house. I'm on the travel site, booking my reservation, saving my window seat, scheduling the travel back for the same day, as per the usual, when my email application dings. The top line in the inbox lit blue. **Reply: Hello! from Shrina L.**

I stare at it for a few minutes. Something about it doesn't look right. I return to the main page, buy the plane ticket, and drag the confirmation email to my "Portland" file.

When I do manage to open the email, the first thing I notice are all the dots from the exclamation marks, like the page is just littered with dots. It is difficult to focus enough to read. She has lived so long and so fully in my memory that it is hard to comprehend that she is also a person in the world, a person capable of receiving an email and replying, ever, not to mention within the hour. She says hello, says she remembers me, of course. That she is so glad to hear from me. She thinks it's so funny that I remember her fringy scarf. She loved that fringy scarf. She asks me if I stayed in Los Angeles, and how I'm doing, and how my mother is doing, and if I became close to the baby who was born right around that time. It's too much. I close the computer screen and leave the apartment.

62

Later, in the darkness of the living room, packages mailed, dinner eaten, the rectangular white screen the only light by which to see, I read the rest. The babysitter tells me how she too remembers that weekend so well. That it has had this hold on her memory, too. How I had said I might burn her with a blowtorch, but it was so sad because I was in such a tough situation and I had never been a mean kid. She says she does have a new cat—she's amazed I remember the name. Hattie died years ago, but he was old and had a happy cat life, and the new one is called Organza and it's a long story why but it fits her perfectly. She says she has often wondered about me and is so very, very glad I wrote. She thanks me many times. She asks me to send on her good wishes to Mrs. Washington, too. She knows everything about that school.

After I read it over a number of times, I press Reply. I type in to Shrina that it is very good to hear from her, too. I tell her that I finished college several years back and am still in Los Angeles, making a living by yard sale purchasing and sending packages through the mail. I tell her my mother is still in a residential facility in Portland, but is doing much better, thank you for asking. I tell her the baby is great, is Vicky, and we get along very well. I compliment her memory. I tell her I too remember saying those frightening things to her, and I apologize. "You apologized at the time!" she writes back, immediately. "You certainly don't need to apologize now." Privately, I think that I did not say the blowtorch part, but I don't add that to the email. We go back and forth a few times, with shorter notes, quicker answers, and then laughing ("haha"), she writes that there is one thing she hasn't mentioned yet that is important to her, and that I might not believe it but she still has that butterfly lamp for me if I want it—"I don't know if you'll remember but you loved this lamp of mine with butterflies all over the shade and we talked about it, and you even asked for it at one point, and I still have it and would be so incredibly pleased if you would accept it as a gift." I tell her I completely remember, and that is very thoughtful of her, but that I am fine with lamps, that I have a durably well-lit room.

Then, some minutes pass, and I reconsider. "You know, I spoke too soon," I write her again in the darkness. "I'd love the lamp. Thank you so much for the offer. May I pay you for it?"

She is so happy. I can feel her happiness on the

screen. She writes how she feels it belonged to me, felt that keenly ever since I'd left, that it had just seemed so wrong in her apartment the minute she returned from the train station that day, like this glaring error, and she had wrapped it up and kept it in the closet and held on to it through several moves just in case maybe someday I would contact her, just like I had. She would mail it to me pronto and please, please, it would be a gift. She says she is so glad I am doing well, and she is now living in Nashville but if I ever want to come out there the music and food are amazing, and it is such an up-and-coming town and she has a guest bed ("Not a loft anymore! A real room to yourself!") and even through the type I can hear her voice lifting. She tells me she's still a teacher but not an aide anymore, now with her own classes of high school English and choir. She also plays out on the weekends with her guitar, singer/songwriter material, but not all that much as she isn't a young pup these days in the music world and the competition is unbelievable. She has a partner, Betsy, and they'd love to see me if and when I ever have a hankering to visit the South.

"Thank you," I write back. "That is so nice, thank you."

63

The routine continues, I box and rebox, visit the post office, tour garage sales, get released by Jose, go see **Our Town,** stand and applaud. I sit in the memory tent early in the mornings but my focus feels different, looser. The canvas starts to peel again a little, on another side, but for whatever reason, it doesn't bother me quite as much. I still zip it up, but mostly out of habit. I reply to a friend who has emailed me a couple times, telling her I'm fine, asking how she is, and on the weekend stop by the building manager's early holiday party, which has, already, four fruitcakes, and where I sit in a chair and hear about how Jose spent the weekend tending to a horse named Kalamazoo, and also from tiny Eleanor in the pale blue turtleneck, who has lived here all her life, and remembers the orange groves, the Lockheed era, and the movie business influx for real.

The package from Nashville arrives on a Tuesday, and I bring it inside and leave it on the floor. Since my apartment remains unfurnished, full instead of all those brown boxes ready to be stuffed and sealed and sent around the world, another brown box is nothing new, is an antelope joining its herd. I put it near the ebony side table I found at a giant moving sale in Hermosa Beach, from four houses on a block trying as a unit to raise money for the local park's baseball team. There's no rush, and no pressure to open it right away, and the only way it asserts its subtle presence in the room as separate from all the other work boxes is due to the babysitter's writing of my address in an orange sparkly pen, with stars and smiley faces around my name.

In early December, I print out my boarding pass and fly up to Portland to see my mother. I arrive around noon, and since she doesn't have a show to prepare for, this time she takes me on a tour of her bedroom, a private room now, with her evening activity planning chart on the wall, her therapy schedule, group and individual, and framed photos of me and Aunt Minn and Uncle Stan and Vicky and Edward all over her dresser. She shows me the various bottles of her meds, and how she keeps track in small colorfully glazed ceramic bowls marked by the days of the week. She loves the scarf gift, and touches it to her cheek; she slides the earrings in immediately, little shimmers on her lobes. We have about four hours together, which we use to walk to the café down the street with the pink glass chandeliers. She will be mailing my gifts, she tells me several times, and I tell her it's no problem, it's my actual job to find these things. Her fingers drift up to the earrings. "Antiques," she says, with wonder.

My flight back is close to six p.m., and as I am getting ready to head to the airport, she threads her arm through mine and clears her throat and tells me that although she has never made it to Los Angeles as she had hoped, this visit she would like to get physically closer to where I am going, as close as she can, so she would like very much this time to accompany me to the airport. Would that be okay? Her gaze is steady. It seems to be something she has rehearsed asking. Sure, I tell her, as we walk to the bus stop together. "You can go right now?" I ask. "I can." There are new truck restaurants across the street, selling empanadas and Thai soups. She holds her purse tight on her shoulder as we step onto the bus. I cannot remember ever being with my mother on any kind of public transportation.

We take the bus to the Red Line, get off at the airport, and split the electric glass doors. There aren't many places a person can go in an airport without a boarding pass, so together we wander the outskirts. Mine, the five-forty, is one of the last Portland–Burbank flights of the day. I ask my mother why she doesn't like to fly, and she tells me it is because she had a dream once, an extremely lucid dream, of a horrifying plane crash. "I know I'm not psychic," she says, shaking her head, "but it really spooked me." We walk into a store and I tell her about how when I was eight, and they needed me to go to L.A., I had refused the plane, too. We are standing by a table full of airport treasures, snow globes, smoked salmon packages, baseball caps and postcards, picking up items, putting them back down. "I always thought the train was Uncle Stan's idea!" she says, delighted. She has never heard this part of the story. She claps her hands. "I thought it was so brilliant because he wanted you to take the transition slowly."

I swirl snow around a tiny Portland's downtown, and tell her no, not his, not at all. That at the time I thought out a plane would be blur, and I couldn't even begin to handle that. She runs her fingers over the bumpy letters of the pulp book titles on the shelves. The airport is already beginning to get to me; I think I can even smell the seeping odor of the word search books in their rows over by the magazines, the extended feel of transition in every item. "When you were very little," my mother says, taking my arm again, "I used to spin you around. You didn't like that either."

"What would I do?"

"You would cry," she says.

"And what would you do?"

She looks at me with surprise. "Honey," she says. "I would stop."

We stroll to the check-in area and get my boarding pass. She watches me do all the parts needed on the computer, and admires my swiftness. She will be taking the Red Line and bus back to the facility, where Edward is waiting. They're helping host another busy night ahead, with karaoke tunes from the decades. This week will be the sixties, and she's especially looking forward to the folk songs.

"Do you remember," I say as we walk to security, "when I told you about that butterfly lamp?"

She glances to the side, watching a family manage their luggage. "Yes," she says, warily.

The intercom announces a flight delay at Gate 18. Not my gate. Far in the distance, we see people running somewhere, late.

"No, don't worry," I say, seeing her tightening, listening, "all I wanted to tell you is that the babysitter sent it to me. That's all. The actual lamp. I wrote her a note. She said she saved it. I haven't opened it yet."

"You found her?"

"Yeah." We step into the security line. She told me she will stand with me all the way to the TSA guard, and then she will duck under the black elastic and exit to the bus stop.

"What was her name again? Sheila?"

"Shrina."

"She was very kind. How is she doing?"

"Sounds like she's doing very well. She lives in Nashville now."

My mother nods a few times, mostly to herself. "Good," she says, absently. "Good."

"She kept it for twenty years," I say.

My mother touches the corner of her eye. We are only a few people from the front of the line. I ask her how the airport visit feels. If it's doing what she'd hoped.

"I don't know," she says. "I'm not sure."

"What did you hope?"

She looks away. Beyond security, the airport widens, full of access to stores and food and seating and windows. After TSA checks me, and my carry-on, and my shoes, I will be going straight to the pretzel stand to get a sourdough pretzel and a lemonade, a plan that is starting to superimpose itself over all the other thoughts in my mind. I will sit on a chair next to strangers and scroll around on my phone.

"It's okay, Mom," I say. "I'll come back soon."

She waves her hands in the air. Her eyes fix on the shrinking line. "I'm glad you were able to contact the babysitter," she says. She speaks clearly, over the tremor in her voice. "Please, thank her for me. I have always very much wanted to thank her. Will you do that?"

"Yes."

She turns to me, and her eyes are bright. "Maybe," she says, "you will have a room full of butterflies when you get home. Flying around your apartment. Wouldn't that be something?"

I smile at her. I have never explained to her how it works.

"Maybe," I say.

The line ends. She ducks under the black elastic, and I step forward. The agent scrutinizes my face, and then hands back my boarding pass and ID.

"Bye," she calls, stepping away before the security guards direct her out.

64

Plane to rideshare to curb to door. The body moves through hundreds of miles, and it's late by the time I get in. Put away my jacket and book, throw out my boarding pass stub, wash hands, brush teeth. The box is where I left it, and easy to slit open with a knife. I imagine my mother's wish, the butterflies filling the room like an animated movie. Inside, the babysitter has carefully wrapped the lamp in several layers of pink tissue paper, which I unroll from the translucent plastic base and shade. She has wrapped it all with such neat corners that it brings me right back to her loft and all the things in it, the oatmeal bowls topped with brown sugar, the lemon verbena in the soap dish, the arranged fringy scarf over the TV.

When the last piece of tissue paper falls away, the smell of dust and aging fabric fills the room. And there it is, the butterfly lamp. I have thought about it, too, in memory-form for so long that it is nothing short of bizarre to encounter in three dimensions.

It is light to hold, and durable. The whole thing is also surprisingly little, and yellower, with the distinct look of the 1980s in the shapes and color scheme, something I didn't realize at all as a child but that marks the babysitter's age and era. I turn it around. Those familiar butterflies, so gilded and red, so slightly stylized and pretend rich-looking, and the gap in the pattern that I can find if I track very carefully.

I spend ten or so minutes with it, but it has no more charge, or mystery, so I bring it to the corner and set it up with a red velvet background, take a few photographs. It's online in twenty minutes, "Butterfly Lampshade from the '80s! Excellent Condition" with a buyer by the end of the hour, Letitia in New York City. She tells me it's so perfect and retro, and that she loves butterflies and finds their symbolism reassuring as she is moving through an important personal transition at this time.

I mail it the following day. Five stars.

65

On Saturday, I get up early and take the bus to my aunt and uncle's house. Aunt Minn is making some kind of egg and green chile dish in the kitchen, and she hoots when she sees me at the door as if I am a surprise celebrity arrival. "Come in!" she says, "what a treat!" At the kitchen counter, she asks about the visit, and I tell her about how my mother looked, and her manner, to which my aunt listens intently, whisking the eggs into a froth. As soon as I can, I head up the stairs to Vicky's room. "You staying for breakfast?" my aunt calls, and I call back, "Sure, if there's enough, if it's okay?" and she makes the irritated grunt she always makes when I act like I am a guest as I have since I moved in, those twenty years ago.

Vicky's on her bed, in her pajamas, reading about the fine art of stage managing. She waves me in and tells me about the final performance of **Our Town,** and how Jordan, her assistant, forgot to bring on the desk, and so the actors had to pretend a desk but they did a really good job and no one in the audience even knew. She shows me a card she's designing as a thank-you for the teacher, an illustration of a porch with the suggestion of something far in the distance. "What does that look like to you?" she asks, pointing at the corner, and I tell her it's not clear, "like something is coming, but nothing ominous." "Good," she says, shading in the background a little more with a pencil. "That's good." We talk a little more about her friends at school, and when there's a natural lull in the conversation I ask her if it would be okay if I could glance at that rose she retrieved so many years ago out of the garbage bin, the one she'd brought over a few months back to inaugurate the tent. "That is, if you don't mind." She gives me a look, the same kind of look that Aunt Minn just did with her voice, and reaches down to open up the drawer and lift it off its slip of satin. It is beige now, now that I let myself look more closely, barely touched with pink anymore, and it looks smaller than before, shrunken by time. Together, we touch its old and weathered petals. For a while it's quiet, just us and the rose, and when it seems like words won't bruise the moment, I fill her in on what I remember of the last stretch of the train ride, including the visitors in their suits, and the beetle, and the giving of the tickets. I tell her my thought about me maybe being a ticket too since I swallowed the butterfly. Then I tell her that the rose is of course hers to do with as she wants;

she rescued it from the green bin, she kept it safe for many years, and if she still wants to keep it for her grandchildren, that is fine. But, I say, for whatever reason, I decided to leave the beetle years ago on a bus. Vicky raises her eyebrows, listening, silent. She runs a fingertip over a cracked petal. "So, where are you a ticket to?" she asks. I laugh a little. I tell her I have no idea. "I mean, I don't even know if it's the right word," I say. "It feels kind of like a bad translation." She looks up at me. "Translation of what?" and we laugh awkwardly together to fill the silence. "You ride the buses," she says. "Yeah." "Are you waiting for someone to come find you?" "No," I say, "I don't think so." "You won't go off with some stranger into another dimension, will you, Francie?" "No," I say, "I live here now." She shakes her head, laughing again. "You say it like you used to live somewhere else, like on some other plane," and I smile at her. What to tell Vicky? She has lived her whole life here.

Later, after egg soufflé, after a round of cards, I say bye and walk a few blocks to the corner to take the 183 back up Magnolia. It's a clear winter Saturday at noon, and the San Gabriel Mountains are visible in the distance, lightly dusted with snow. The bus driver hums at the stoplights. At home, I return to my closet and pull out the purple knapsack that once held the beetle, and put it, with its old word searches and broken tape recorders, into the garbage.

I go to the balcony and with hammers and a saw, disassemble the tent, carrying the canvas and the wooden beams to the trash bin downstairs.

"Redecorating?" asks the building manager, poking her head out the window, and I tell her yes, sure, good idea.

She's right that without the tent, there's a fair amount of new room on the balcony, so the next day at the supermarket, at my weekly grocery shop, I get another succulent, and on the walk home pass a yard sale I'd seen listed earlier, which has two decent-looking wicker plastic chairs and a plastic table and a seller willing to drive them over. They look nice on the balcony, facing out, the little plastic table between, so I text Vicky to invite her to come over and take a look. To say goodbye to the tent she helped build. She writes back right away, with a surprise face. You're getting a lot done this weekend! she writes, and then tells me she's just sitting around ruining her drawing, and that she'll be right over.

When she arrives, she calls out from downstairs, over by the trash bins.

"I'm here!" she says, standing on the bricks. "I can see it!"

From the balcony's edge, I can glimpse her profile peering at the tent's deconstructed shape, orange canvas and wooden beams now stacked against spilled bags of lemon rinds and carrot peels, leaky milk cartons and a pair of old ripped black socks.

She is holding a bag of cookies in her hand. She looks so young in the world, so ready to leave this city and make her own. When she runs up the stairs and into my apartment, she goes straight to the balcony and stands right where the tent was. "Don't you miss it already?" she asks, closing her eyes. I bring out a plate for the cookies and make her some kind of juice and sparkling water concoction, and we settle into the chairs, use the table for our snacks. Cars trundle along the streets below. I tell her it's a little too soon to tell, but my guess is that I will miss it, and also won't, and that there will always be plenty more to remember, but that it seemed like the right time to take it down, at least for now; I did the course, I tell her: I started when my mother smashed her hand, and I ended at the doorstep in Burbank, and in that way I made the journey over again, from one family to another. I glance over at her. It's almost evening, and the air is chilly, and she's wrapped in a blanket, staring out at the streets, with a light dusting of cookie crumbs at the fabric's edge. She was just that baby when I met her. She had those golden eyes, even then, and she would coo at me, and Aunt Minn told me once, in the hallway, pulling me aside, that Vicky cooed at me more than she cooed at anyone. I told Uncle Stan in the school office by the cluster of secretaries that I could not take the plane, and he'd nodded, because the world would've been a blur, and so he bought me a train ticket to slow it down, and in the tent, I slowed it down again. I slowed it way down. I looked at it all as slowly as I could.

When it was time to apply to college, my mother had hoped I might return to Portland, this time on my own, by choice, to be near her, and to learn and study at Reed, or Lewis & Clark, or Portland State, or Pacific U. But I didn't apply anywhere outside Los Angeles, and I ended up going to UCLA. I told her it was because I wanted to be near Vicky, which was mostly true. There were shows to see. There were essays to edit. I stayed, and did my time in the dorm, and took my classes, and ate the weekly dinners in Burbank, and graduated, and found my own apartment nearby. Soon, though, Vicky will be leaving the city, and my stated reason and excuse for staying will be gone. But I want to live here, now, no question, in the valley by the mountains, Vicky or no Vicky, heat-blasted or cold. I am comfortable here. I have made here my home, just as my mother did with Portland.

At the airport, before she left, my mother gripped my hand and looked at me closely, like she was trying to give me something with her eyes. She was having her own experience, her own reasons for things, but it did register to me, to have her there with me at the airport. She had never been with me at any kind of way station before; I had never had her with me as I prepared to get on yet another mode of transportation, her the person at the side, waving goodbye, as we split and our dots on the map moved elsewhere, apart. The airport, as always, filled me with that vague queasiness, as I passed through the identification checkpoint and stood in line to take off my shoes. She walked to where they would let her stand, still waving, on the side by the donut counter and the trinket store. My security line shuffled forward. An agent directed me to the screening machine, and my bags passed through the X-ray devices. I couldn't see her for a few minutes, and when I was able to check again, I found her in the far distance, stepping through the space between the electric doors, into the evening air.

"All clear," said the agent, moving on to the next person.

There was all my stuff on the conveyor belt, waiting to be claimed. I put my shoes back on and slipped on my jacket. I shouldered my backpack and picked up my purse. Then I headed over to the gate with all of it to wait for the flight home.

ABOUT THE AUTHOR

AIMEE BENDER is the author of the novels **The Particular Sadness of Lemon Cake**—a **New York Times** bestseller—and **An Invisible Sign of My Own,** and of the collections **The Girl in the Flammable Skirt, Willful Creatures,** and **The Color Master**. Her works have been widely anthologized and have been translated into sixteen languages. She lives in Los Angeles.